After
THE LAST
Fall

After THE LAST Fall

amy babiarz

THE UNBOUND PRESS

ISBN: 978-1-913590-09-3

The Unbound Press
www.theunboundpress.com

Hey unbound one!

Welcome to this magical book brought to you by The Unbound Press.

At The Unbound Press we believe that when women write freely from the fullest expression of who they are, it can't help but activate a feeling of deep connection and transformation in others. When we come together, we become more and we're changing the world, one book at a time!

This book has been carefully crafted by both the author and publisher with the intention of inspiring you to move ever more deeply into who you truly are.

We hope that this book helps you to connect with your Unbound Self and that you feel called to pass it on to others who want to live a more fully expressed life.

With much love,
Nicola Humber

Founder of The Unbound Press

www.theunboundpress.com

For Spencer

Who Has Been There Since the Beginning

_"Let it be known and declared that a new dynasty has usurped the Tumis Dynasty.

Let it be known and declared that a new order has been set forth. Let it be known and declared that the old laws have been stricken in favor of the law of the Raznik Dynasty. Failure to follow the letter of the law will result, without question, in the imprisonment and execution of those who deign to break with our new order.

1) There is to be no new trade with courts outside of our own. We will grow from our land, build from our land, and carry our people through into a new order. Battlewood is an independent court, sustainable and free from reliance on those around us. If you are found to be trading, you will be punished.

2) There is to be no communication with courts outside of our own. Battlewood does not allow room for governmental overthrows or for seeds of dissent to be planted. The law set forth by the Raznik Dynasty is resolute. If you are found to be communicating, you will be punished.

3) There is to be no magic of any kind. Magic is a dark practice unsupported by our lands. It is the decision of this court moving forward that any magic of any kind will result in execution. Battlewood needs no magic, nor does it support the worship of falsehoods or idols. If anyone is found to be in possession of these evil relics, or to be partaking in this practice, they will be sentenced to execution, with no room for mercy.

Let your lives be guided from this moment forward by the Raznik Dynasty. We will move our people into greatness. We will not allow for missteps or crime. Those who show themselves to be the weak links of our society will be dealt with accordingly. The Raznik Dynasty intends to lead our people with steadfast determination and victory.

Further, let it be known that, henceforth, Battlewood has entered into a Pact of Silence with our neighboring courts.

Battlewood and its people belong to the Raznik Dynasty.

Do not falter."

-from "A New Land". Issued on the third day of the month Knin in the year E3.

ONE
E103

I am awakened by the sounds of the front door breaking open. I leap out of my bed, reaching under the frame to grab my weapon. All that I can see in the darkness is the flicker of lanterns and the glint of steel. Still half-blind and -deaf from sleep, I cannot make out what is unfolding before me. Someone lights a fire in the hearth and within a moment, the room lights up with the flames. Warriors, in my home, at some ungodly hour. They overturn my books and papers without care. Pots, pans, and dishes clatter to the floor as they pull my belongings off of their shelves and out of their cupboards. I will my senses to sharpen as I take in the scene before me. Behind the three warriors, I see that my door hangs on its hinges, splintered and cracked.

"You know, a simple knock would have been just as effective," I tell them. I have not lowered my weapon. "Would anyone care to tell me what this is about, or do you just intend to go on disrupting my kitchen?"

"Unless you have something helpful to say, shut up," the largest of the three says.

"Well, maybe I have," I say, "but it seems that you've all neglected to tell me why you've broken into my home in the middle of the night."

"Are you alone?" one of them, a woman, asks me.

"Except for my sister, yes." I look over to Aleca's bed to point her out, and then freeze. Her bed is empty. Again. "Damn her," I mutter.

"Where is she?"

"Given that I thought she was here and that I was asleep when you arrived, I haven't a clue," I say. "Why are you looking for her?"

"If you are hiding her," the woman tells me, "we will find out."

They leave without another word and I stand in the middle of the mess, watching their retreating backs. Not even a full minute later, Aleca sprints in through the door and presses herself into the shadows.

"Are they gone?" she asks, breathless.

"Any interest in telling me what that was about?" I ask in response.

"You don't have to worry about it," she retorts.

I move toward her, pulling her out of the shadows. "No," I tell her, "you don't get to decide that. I can't keep covering for you if you're going to keep being so reckless!" She rolls her eyes and I give her a little shake. "Warriors broke in here tonight looking for you, Aleca. Do you know what that could mean for you, or for both of us? We could have been arrested, or killed."

"You're being dramatic, Jace," Aleca tells me, stifling a yawn.

"You're being an idiot, Aleca," I spit back. "Go to bed, and don't let me find your bed empty again." She does so without argument and, within moments, I hear the sounds of her breathing even out. She has been taking off more and more often, lately. At first, I thought it was a phase, but now...now, I'm not so sure.

I spend the night cleaning up the mess made by the warriors. Several of the books have been ruined and I throw them into the fire. I am just finishing the clean-up when the first light of morning begins to filter through the windows. Aleca snores lightly from her bed, unbothered. I throw a shoe at her and she wakes up, spluttering.

"What was that for?" she cries.

"Wake up," I tell her. "You're not wasting your day just because you wanted to go adventuring in the middle of the night. I took care of it last night, but I'm not doing it again. Seriously, Al, what is going on with you?" She rubs blearily at her eyes, and I'm not certain a single word I've said has registered with her. I loft the other shoe at her. "Aleca! Wake up!"

"I'm awake!" she protests.

"Good. Go to your classes, keep your head down, and don't do anything that will draw more attention to you today," I tell her. "We are under Raznik's eye as it is. Do you know what it looks like when my own troop comes bursting into our house, trying to catch us doing something illegal?" She does not move and I stride over to her bed. In one motion, I scoop her out of the bed and dump her onto the ground. She jumps up, tangled in her blankets, and lets out a shout at me. I ignore her and point at her clothes hanging on the wall. With a grumble, she snatches them off of their hooks and stomps behind a changing screen. I sigh and begin to pack up my food for the day. My patience has worn out with my little sister, and though I love her dearly, I could cheerfully kill her. I have worked hard to get to where I am in our band of warriors, and she puts that at risk each and every time she sneaks away in the dead of night.

The moment she is ready, I march her to the school and shove her into her seat. I reiterate the warning from this morning and she mock-salutes me.

"Don't be a brat," I tell her. Softening, I say, "Let's do something together tonight, yeah? Just you and me, a sisters' night." She grumbles but nods, and I ruffle her hair. "Make good choices."

I make my way down to our training field. Galter and Rolf, two of my team, are there waiting for our captain, Linota. I join them and they eye me knowingly.

"Long night, huh?" Rolf asks me. I make a face at him and shake my head.

"She doesn't understand the implications of what she is doing, and I can't get her to listen to me," I say. "I don't know what else to do." I wrap my wrists and hands tightly with leather, preparing for our day.

"Don't be too hard on yourself, Grimme," Galter tells me. "We all know that you're trying. We know you. You've made some bad choices in the past, but Linota doesn't take on just anyone." I run a hand over my face, masking my exhaustion as I yawn. It will not do for me to sleep through my training.

"Look alive, kiddos!" Linota booms. She strides down the hill toward our training enclosure and hoists herself over the fence. Not wasting a moment, she begins putting us through the wringer. I am pouring sweat in no time. I take out my frustrations at my sister on a dummy until the dingy canvas busts open and old straw falls out. I feel the anger bleed out of me with each hit. "Well done," Linota says, clapping a hand on my shoulder. "Do it again."

I am steered to another dummy. This one is also canvas but filled with a firm stuffing, more like a human. I hit over and over again, undercut, uppercut, and everything in between. My hands are throbbing by the end of the exercise and my knuckles bloom with bruises.

The day continues like this. I am barely able to move by the end but I will not allow myself to stop. I know that the moment I do, my exhaustion will take over and I will not be able to move again. All of my frustrations are taken out on the dummies and released during our mock-fights. My muscles are screaming by the time the sun is setting. Galter and Rolf each thump me on the back as we part ways and I turn to make my way back home.

Before I have made it out of the training enclosure, a shadow falls over me. I look up and into the eyes of one of Raznik's guards, Ocin. A mean, feral smile breaks out on his face and he crosses his arms, tutting. I stare at him silently as I wait for him to speak. When he doesn't, I raise my eyebrow, pointedly.

"Do you need something, or are you just practicing for your prestigious role of standing outside of a door all day?" I ask him. I try to move past him and he moves with me to block my way again. "Seriously, Ocin? Speak, or get out of my way."

"You've got a lot to say for someone who is in deep water," he tells me. "Had any visitors recently?" I set my jaw and glare at him. When he realizes that I am not taking his bait, the smile drops and he uncrosses his arms. "I've been ordered to bring you to our Commander. Must have done something pretty bad, if he wants to see you."

With a groan, I turn on my heel and stare up the steep hill to the castle where Raznik lives. I don't know how I'm going to make my bone-tired body carry me up there, but it doesn't seem that I have an option. This, without a doubt, has to do with Aleca. I'm going to kill her.

...... † ......

When we arrive at the castle, Aleca is standing in the entry hall with a guard. Her wrists are bound behind her back in iron cuffs and I let out an indignant sound. She looks down at the ground and whispers something. I move closer, trying to hear her. Desnal, the guard she is with, speaks over her, "What the brat is trying to tell you is that she's been arrested and is going before the court when the sun reaches its height tomorrow."

"On what grounds?" I ask furiously.

"Treason, immoral practice, being a Grimme…take your pick," he says. "Let's get going; our Commander doesn't like to be kept waiting."

"Don't be frightened," I try to comfort Aleca as we are led down a dim hallway. We are sandwiched between Desnal and Ocin—a reminder that the only place to go is forward, toward an uncertain future. Of all of the times I have been in a tight spot before, I have never felt this fear of the unknown and, with it, the knowledge that this could be the end of life as I've come to know it. I fight off a shudder of fear.

"I'm not frightened." Despite her defiant bravado, I see her bottom lip quiver. The flickering candles on the wall throw our faces into grotesque relief. It does not prevent me from seeing the nervousness on her face. All of my anger from earlier has melted away; gnawing guilt fills the void. I give her hand a small squeeze in a silent apology—I'm sorry that I failed you. I'm sorry that I couldn't protect you.

"Quiet!" one of the guards barks at us. We fall silent again. Aleca casts her eyes downward. I have to bite my tongue to stop me from lashing out at the guard. It is my fault Aleca is here. I was bound to protect her, and I failed. I should have corralled her better. I should have burned her notes. There are so many things that I should have done differently.

"Jace," she whispers, glancing nervously at the guards, "take this." She rattles her chains just enough for me to realize that she's holding something. I reach over quickly and then place my hands at my side again. I clutch a folded scrap of parchment and run a thumb over it before shoving it into the waistband of my pants. Aleca looks straight ahead again and says nothing else.

We come to a stop in front of heavy oak doors, and a guard raises a fist to knock. Commander Raznik's voice calls, "Enter!" and the doors are opened. We are escorted in. Raznik is lounging before the massive fireplace, crystal tumbler in hand. He sips his brown liquor lazily, not bothering to look at us. "That will be all, guards."

"Sir," they say in unison before backing out of the room. The door is closed behind us. The crackling and spitting of the fire fills the silence. Aleca and I stand motionless, waiting. Raznik downs the rest of his drink in one gulp and finally rises.

"Ah, the sisters Grimme," he drawls. Aleca and I exchange a look and then stare at Raznik. "You two have proven to be nothing but trouble. I expected more from you." He turns his back on us to refill his glass. "You know, Jace, when we agreed to take you on as a warrior, we thought that meant the end of your days as resident rebel."

"It wasn't–," Aleca begins. I elbow her hard and she falls silent.

"And you, Aleca...I never thought I would see the day that you broke a rule, and here you've broken the biggest law of them all!" He makes his way back to the leather chair and then motions to the ottoman across from it. "Sit."

"No, thank you," I say stiffly. "We prefer to stand." Raznik raises an eyebrow at me but does not fight it.

"As you wish," he says, sipping slowly as he stares. "Such a pity–"

"Why have you called us here?" I cut in. "Aleca is to be tried in sixteen hours. She should be with her family."

"Oh, but she is," Raznik says, motioning to me. "In fact...she's here because of her family."

"How dare-!"

"Enough," he asserts. "The fact is that you have information that I want, Aleca. It is no secret to me that you have been ferreting away to cross the borders. Oh, yes, I know all about your midnight excursions," he adds at in response to the expression of shock on her face. "And I know that you helped her, Jace, even if we cannot prove it."

Aleca and I do not dare to look at each other as he speaks. We both know that he is telling the truth. I knew that I should have done more to prevent her; my other option, though, would be to allow her to navigate unsafely and potentially be killed in the process. I couldn't let that happen.

"So what is it you're looking for?" Aleca asks carefully.

"I'm offering you both your freedom—at a small price," Raznik says. He sips his drink, and the glass throws a glint of light as the flames reflect off of it. "Aleca, all I ask of you is that you hand over the information you've collected about our neighboring courts. I know you've learned about them, and I want what you know."

"And how exactly do I fit into this?" I ask.

"Isn't that obvious?" Raznik asks in surprise. "I want you to help me invade their land. Jace, we both know that your, shall we say, unsavory history lends itself to this task."

"I gave that up months ago," I say angrily. "I told you I wouldn't go back."

"Not even to save your own family? It's not so hard to fall back into old habits, is it?" When I do not respond, Raznik's mouth curves into a smirk. I clench my jaw and look away, unable to withstand the smugness pouring from him. "Would you like a drink?" he offers suddenly, motioning to his drink cart. My fingers twitch with a sudden desire to hit him and I ball my fists tightly behind my back. The motion does not go unnoticed by Raznik. His smirk widens.

"I won't give you a thing," Aleca says defiantly. "I...I couldn't, even if I wanted to."

"And why is that?" he asks through gritted teeth.

"I burned my notes," she says with a shrug. "They're gone. Well, I wasn't going to let someone like you take hold of them, was I?"

Raznik narrows his eyes at Aleca, then at me, then her again, trying to determine the validity of her words. I give a shrug of my own—I don't know what she's done with them—and he turns his back on us.

"You're even more useless to this land than I thought," he spits out. "Get out of my sight. Aleca Grimme, you are to be tried in sixteen hours for treason against Battlewood. Expect no mercy."

...... † ......

Aleca has been secured deep within the confines of the castle dungeons. I have been given five minutes alone with her before her solitary confinement begins. She seems unaffected by the trial looming over her. I, on the other hand, am a bundle of nerves; I feel as if I could snap at any moment. There are less than sixteen hours standing between us and a decision that could leave me entirely without a family. We've already lost our parents—I cannot lose my sister, too.

As soon as the guard has slammed the gate shut, I run over to Aleca and throw my arms around her. She hugs me back tightly.

"I'm sorry, Aleca," I tell her. "I should have been able to prevent this from happening. I knew what you were up to, but I—"

"Hush, Jace," Aleca replies. "I did this to myself, and I would do it again. Raznik can do whatever he wants to me." She walks over to the gate to check for guards and then rushes back over to me. "I didn't burn my notes," she whispers quickly. "I've hidden them. I need you to find them and keep them safe for me, until I can get out."

"What are you talking about, get out? Aleca, you're being watched by three guards. How exactly do you intend to escape?"

"It doesn't matter," she says. "And anyway, the less you know, the better. If anyone asks you anything, you won't have to lie. Why are you looking at me like that?"

"I'm just trying to figure out where my little sister has gone," I say. "You used to be so quiet and mild-mannered, and now you're plotting...well, something."

"And you used to be a delinquent drunk," Aleca reminds me. "We aren't who we used to be." She is quiet for a moment, and then says, "Jace, whatever happens...I love you. You're the best sister I could have ever hoped for." She throws her arms around me again and I can feel her sniffle against my shoulder, showing me a crack in her façade.

"I love you too," I whisper, stroking her hair. "I'll do whatever it takes to keep you safe."

"Time's up!" a guard's voice booms. The gate creaks open, and I'm escorted out of the cell. As the door slams, I catch one last glimpse of my sister through the bars before I am pushed around the corner and out of sight.

······ † ······

I cannot sleep. I pace endlessly in the space that Aleca and I once shared. Of course, I have been alone now for several weeks; my sister's trips have grown more and more frequent in recent days. Aleca is planning something, and I have no idea what it could be. She intends to break out of the dungeons, but how? I have stood guard at those dungeons, and I know them better than my own home. There is no way that she can escape unharmed. Unless…

I shake my head. Aleca is foolhardy, but even she could not be stupid enough to break out with the one thing that got her locked up in the first place.

I take a shuddering breath. I cannot calm myself, and I cannot stop thinking about Aleca locked up in the cold dungeons. Having spent a night or two there myself as a prisoner, I know just how cold they can be, even on a warm day like today. There is no concern that water drips through the crevices of the stone walls, or that the chilly draft comes through to extinguish the flames of the torches on the wall—the only real source of heat for the prisoners. There is no concern that spiders, rats, and other scuttling critters go running unchecked. You are there to learn a lesson—your age does not matter. Battlewood is an unforgiving land. Or, rather, Battlewood will forgive only once you've been made to suffer.

Confusion, fear, anger, and sadness all battle to reign

superior in my head. I am confused by my sister—this Aleca is not the sweet lamb I spent my years chasing around while she grew. The cool, shrewd Aleca who faced down Raznik is someone entirely foreign to me. I am worried about her. I do not know what will happen at her trial; I have a good idea, though. The thought of losing yet another family member leaves me empty and despairing, without direction.

Unable to pace anymore, I distract myself by packing and re-packing my bags. I have been trained to keep packs filled and prepared for a moment's notice. There is not much to pack, but I do so anyway. I fold my clothing methodically over and over again until the creases and folds are just right. I take stock of the dried meats and fruits, the soup balls, the teas. I clean my portable pans and cups until the metal shines and reflects my face back to me.

It is only as I reach for my blade that I remember the note I have tucked into my waistband. I pull it out and unfold it quickly, tearing it slightly in my haste. Aleca's careful handwriting fills the page.

"Jace,

My notes are in our old hideaway. Remember how you used to leave me treats there? I loved when you did that. It was like magic. Whatever you do, do not let Raznik find my notes. I know that what I have done is against the law, but I don't care. Someone has to be the first one to try to fix things. If anything happens to me, I need you to make me a promise. I need you to keep doing what I've started. We've been lied to, Jace.

     Always your sister,
       Aleca."

I read the note over and over again. The words are imprinted in my mind, even when I close my eyes. "We've been lied to, Jace." At some point, my eyes do not open, and I fade into a fitful sleep.

······ † ······

"Let's go."

I'm pushed roughly through the door, onto the balcony which overlooks the chamber. It is cold and drab; the only source of color comes from a mosaic inlay of our coat-of-arms on the center of the floor. On all sides, dark marble benches rise in tiers, matching the curve of the chamber. They are empty now, but not for long. One by one, the torches on the walls are lit, casting misshapen shadows. I find I am struggling to swallow properly.

The room begins to fill; with the people comes a cacophony of excited chatter and laughter. This is just another show to them. As I move forward to look over the balcony, the same hands that guided me through the door shove me into a cold marble seat. A man comes to stand next to me, watching the scene in front of us.

"It's quite the turnout, wouldn't you agree?" Commander Raznik asks quietly. There is grim satisfaction in his voice; I do not need to look at him to know that his grizzled face is marked with a smirk. He rests one hand on my left shoulder, and its weight is almost too much to bear. I say nothing and stare straight ahead. Dread fills my veins like acid, and I feel the heat of it flush my face. "It's almost a shame we have to meet like this today. Almost." He removes his hand from my shoulder and steps forward. He raises his arms and calls the court to attention.

"Battlewood, I greet you!" Commander Raznik shouts. The chamber instantly falls silent and the people stare at Raznik with rapt attention. "We gather today under tragic circumstances. We have been betrayed by one of our own." The crowd murmurs and hisses its disapproval. "When one becomes treasonous, we all become treasonous!" At this, the murmurs swell into an angry roar. Raznik holds up his hands, and the crowd quiets again. My heart beats painfully fast against my breastbone.

"The Council has given their time and energy, fought to decide what to make of our betrayer. Do we spare them, and show our mercy, as we have done in years past? Or do we make an example of them, and remind our citizens that there is no higher crime than to go against the ways of your people?"

Simultaneous shouts of, "Spare them!" and "Kill them!" ring

out, echoing off of the walls. I feel I shall go deaf with the sounds, and I know that, regardless of the outcome, I will forever hear the cries of my people calling for my sister's death. Raznik allows the shouting for a few moments and turns to face me with a cruel smirk. I lock eyes with him for only a moment before he turns back to face the crowd.

"Battlewood forgives," he yells, his voice oddly triumphant, "but it never forgets! Therefore, the Council has voted that Aleca Grimme be put to death for the charges of conspiracy and treason!"

My litany of expletives is drowned out by the uproar that breaks from the crowd. They are on their feet, calling, whooping, and laughing. Raznik turns his back to the crowd and beckons to someone in the shadows. They step forward, and into the light.

"Valkyrie Elouned," Raznik says, bowing his head.

"Raznik," she greets in her cold voice, adjusting the jewel-encrusted armor on her fingertips. She is dressed in her ceremonial execution gown and headdress, and the light glints angrily off of the metallic feathers draped from her neck across her right shoulder. My mouth goes dry as she reaches over her left shoulder and unhitches her blade. It is a sepiwin, the traditional weapon of Battlewood. The blade is curved in the shape of an S, the edges sharpened and precise. Elouned grips the leather-wrapped middle and saunters forward.

"We are ready?" she asks, fixing her stare first on me, and

then on Raznik.

"We are," he confirms. She gives one curt nod, steps to the edge of the balcony, and takes flight; ash-colored wings erupt as she leaps. She circles the chamber twice and then comes to the center, landing on the mosaic.

"It is time!" she shouts, lifting her sepiwin high in the air. The crowd erupts again, cheering her on. As she incites them further, the doors to the chamber fly open. Two guards run in, shouting. Their words are unintelligible in the din.

"Silence!" Raznik commands. "What is it, Ocin?"

"The prisoner, sir. She's gone!" Ocin calls.

"What do you mean, 'she's gone?' How can she be gone?" Raznik asks, snarling.

"She's just...gone, sir," Ocin says, shrugging as he struggles to catch his breath. "She was there this morning, and then we went to retrieve her and–"

"–her cell was empty, her cuffs were broken open!" the other guard, Desnal, finishes. "We looked for her all over, I swear, but–"

"I will deal with you two later," Raznik says. His face is red with fury. "Get out of my sight." Rounding on me, he says, "You. What did you do?"

"I have done nothing, Commander. You saw to that when you placed my sister in solitary," I spit. We glare at each other as he clenches and unclenches his jaw, thinking quickly.

"You are going to fix this. You are going to find her, and you are going to bring her back here, alive. And when you do, we will finish what was started. Failure to do so will result in your deaths. Both of you. We will find you, should you not return." Without another word, he sweeps past me and slams the door shut.

I watch from my seat as Valkyrie Elouned circles the chamber like a restless wildcat, angry at the loss of her prey. Her ash wings are still spread wide.

"Aleca," I whisper. "Run."

after the last fall

TWO

I have been given precisely two hours to gather my weapons, clothing, and rations before I become an outlaw in my own land. Once my mark is up, I am fair game. I do not want to be around to find out what that will mean for me. I make quick work of our house. It is a small home, large enough for our family, but nothing of note. I spent years trying to get away from it, trying to spend my time anywhere but there. Now that I am preparing to leave, however, it is as if a hole has opened in my chest. I may not have had a happy adolescence, but it is where all of my memories rest regardless. It is where I grew up.

I wander through the hallway, stopping at each room on my way out. I cannot stall any longer. Grabbing my pack, I give a cursory sweep of the room I once shared with Aleca, and my eyes come to rest on a piece of crinkled paper—Aleca's note. I cannot let Raznik get his hands on it. I hold the note over the flame of a candle until it has turned to ash. With a sigh, I blow out the candle and the room goes dark.

On my way to the castle, I make a detour to the large tree where Aleca and I used to climb and play. All of my memories come rushing back. The presents I would leave here for my little sister: tasty cakes and fizzy drinks; maps leading her to buried treasure; and letters from long-lost ancestors. There was a time when there was no greater honor than to be her big sister. It is only fitting that Aleca has instructed me to find her notes and take them away from this land.

The tree, large and gnarled, hosts a number of hollows in the trunk and I root around the largest of them. Beneath the rotting leaves and broken stems, my fingers touch upon crinkling papers and a leather-bound book. I quickly shove them into my bag, an odd feeling of triumphant foreboding in my chest.

I meet Commander Raznik in the entrance hall of Battlewood Castle. He stands silently, watching me as I approach. When I reach him, he steps forward, hands held out to me. I do not take them. Despite his act, we are nothing more than bitter enemies now.

"Jace," he says. "It is unfortunate, these terms on which we must part. Battlewood values their warriors, and you were among the young we looked forward to having serve for years to come." He pauses, possibly waiting for a response from me. I want to point out that they are his terms on which we are parting, but I do not speak. "Serve Battlewood well, and bring Aleca back to us. Her death is your pardon. You will do this,

Jace. It is not an option. Failure will result in the execution of you and your sister—after we have finished torturing you both. Elouned is very keen to get her hands on you. Do you understand me?"

"Yes, Commander." There is acid in my voice. Surely he cannot truly believe that I would bring my sister home to be murdered? Could I, to save my own life?

"Good. From this point onwards, you are on your own. I await your return." He nods to me before walking up the staircase leading to his chambers. I watch him go, hatred rising in my throat like bile. I cannot believe that I ever looked up to this man, trusted him. At one time, I even considered him my rescuer. And now…now, I cannot feel anything except disgust and contempt. I turn on my heel and exit the castle. As soon as I have crossed the bridge, I hear the sound of it being pulled up, cutting me off from the castle built into the karstic caves of Battlewood. I pause for a moment and then continue down the path.

I do not look back again.

...... † ......

I do not hurry my departure out of Battlewood. I am well aware that Raznik will have placed a bounty on my head if I fail, but it doesn't bother me. Part of me knows that Commander Raznik expects me—expects us both—to come back alive. No one would be foolish enough to kill me before that can happen, though I cannot say the same for whomever I may meet once I am out of Battlewood, and thus out of my court. I quell the fear of what awaits me beyond my land. This is not the first journey I have taken, but it is nothing like the jaunts I have gone on in the past. There is far more at stake this time; if I succeed, one of my family members will die. If I do not succeed, we both die—after we are tortured first. This is, of course, assuming that I do not die trying to find Aleca.

From where I stand, I have a vantage point. On a clear day like today, it is possible to see for miles. To the west, there are green rolling hills and charcoal-grey karstic caves that give way to snow-capped mountains. It is from these caves that I have been cast out. To the east, the land slopes down and becomes a labyrinth of rocks, streams, rivers, and waterfalls. I steel my nerve and set eastward. Plenty of men and women before me, warriors and civilians, have met their demise by not giving this land its due respect, and I hope that I do not become one of them.

I move steadily, following the trail that twists through the hills. It is a well-trodden path, one that I have followed time and again with Aleca in tow. I wonder if she took this path when she fled Battlewood. I also wonder if Raznik is aware that there is every chance that he is sending me to death. It is impossible to know what awaits me beyond the border of Battlewood. It's been nearly a century since Battlewood and the adjoining court, Garyn, were on speaking terms. There is no telling how a citizen of Battlewood will be welcomed into their lands, particularly a warrior. History tells us that Garyn is a sworn enemy of Battlewood.

Although we entered into a time of silence between the other courts a hundred years ago, it has not stopped the animosity between us. A large portion of our warriors have been dispatched throughout the courts in a stealth operation. They report back to Raznik, and what he chooses to do with that information is kept secret. What we do know is that there is something that Raznik, and his predecessors, are trying desperately to keep out of our court. It is also the exact thing that my little sister has decided she wants to pursue, which has made life a real headache for me.

It is the tradition of Battlewood that, prior to a child beginning their education for any trade, they must first learn the history of Battlewood. Before we are even old enough to hold a pen, we learn to cite the motto of Battlewood on command: "Through struggle we persevere, steadfast we conquer." Those who do not know it are subjected to the Commander's wrath. We are also taught to understand that this history is our truth and that there is no other truth. Battlewood is a proud land. I sometimes wonder if it is not our pride that is our downfall. It is also because of our pride that I have to question whether the history we get have been taught is the history that actually happened. Battlewood does not like to be questioned, and if one is wise, they do not question their land or their history. Neither Aleca nor I have ever claimed to be wise. Pig-headed, yes, but not wise. Of course, it is because of this that we are in our current situation.

Soon, the sky begins to darken with the onset of night. The contrast that the setting sun casts between the green of the hills and the darkness of the caves is stunning. The weight of the day begins to settle, and I am hit with the realization that I no longer have a place in the land that was once my home and sanctuary; I am watching the sun set as a stranger in familiar lands. I always assumed I would be banished from my land, but now it is a reality and it feels somehow worse than I expected it would. I focus on finding a place to sleep for the night to distract myself from my reality. I am close to the ravines and water, but would not make it there before dark. Instead, I get myself as close to the water as I possibly can and settle beneath a large linden tree.

My attempts to distract myself last night have paid off-with all the packing I did, I am relatively well-stocked with small cloth balls filled with dry soups, portable cooking ware, and dried meats, vegetables, and fruits. While I know that these supplies will not last forever, they will get me through the next few days, until I can find other sources of food and water. I start a small fire and dump the contents of a soup ball into a small copper pot filled with water. I'm grateful that I have been cast out in the summer: the evening and nighttime temperature does not dip too far. These are small victories, but I must cling to them. The alternative is too much to bear.

With my soup ready and camp laid out, I sit with my back against the trunk of the linden tree. The sun is almost completely set behind the mountains, and the twinkling stars puncture the indigo sky. I peel off my leather riding boots, dip into my bag, and withdraw a bottle of juniper mead. I swiped the drink from my cabinet before I left, as a gift to myself. It has been quite some time since I last had a drink, and I think that, given the circumstances, I deserve this. I finish my soup and then lean back against the tree. One leg straight in front of me, I bend my other leg up and balance my arm on my knee; the bottle dangles against my shin, its neck between my pointer and middle fingers.

Silence has never bothered me, but tonight it feels oppressive. I am acutely aware that it is silent because I am an outcast, because I have no one now. I take a deep swig of the drink, grimacing at the sweet burn of it. Eventually, I feel my eyes begin to droop with fatigue and alcohol. I cork the bottle back up and slip into my bedroll. Aided by the juniper mead, I fall asleep quickly and soundly.

...... † ......

Morning finds me clutching my head and regretting the mead from the night before. I remember hearing my father once say that one should not fight fire with fire, unless that fire is mead. I do not know if he was serious, but I am willing to try anything to cease the pounding in my temples. Popping the cork back out of the bottle, I bring it to my mouth. My stomach roils as the smell of alcohol fills my nose, and before I can retch, I take a large gulp. After a few more gulps, my head seems to ache less, and I sigh with relief. Apparently, my father was right.

I walk slowly for a while, occasionally drinking from the bottle. It is not a bad way to adventure, and I wonder why I have not done so before. I enjoy walking with a light bounce in my step and a general acceptance of the world around me. I do not usually feel this way about my surroundings. I make a note to travel this way more often. I did not, however, consider the fact that once I was away from the caves, it would be considerably warmer. I assume that the mead has also lent a hand in my rising body temperature. The initially enjoyable walk through the hilly land quickly becomes less and less enjoyable as the heat continues to intensify.

By the time the sun hangs high above me, I have shed my leather riding jacket and long-sleeved cotton tunic, leaving me in my cotton riding pants, leather boots, and a sleeveless tank. I wish to take my boots off and walk barefoot in the lush green grass of the hills, but I refrain. In any other circumstance, I would roam the grass openly, enjoying the feeling of it tickling my toes, and the sun-warmed soil coating the soles of my feet. It is a feeling I associate with my family, with our summer picnics—back when I had a family of which to speak. Now, I am on my own.

Soon, the green grass of the hills begins to give way to rocks and dirt as the path leads into Straup Forest. Beyond the forest is Devent Gorge. It is this gorge that serves as the border between Battlewood and Garyn. The realization brings me to my senses, and I take a sip of mead. Whether it is a headache or the impending reality which I am trying to keep at bay, I cannot be sure. I take a deep breath to renew my determination and then set forth into the forest. I am swallowed completely by the shrubs and trees quickly, cutting me off from any view I had left of my old home.

The sun becomes a hazy green light that filters through the trees. I draw my sepiwin and carry it loosely, in case something, or someone, unexpectedly makes an appearance. I forge through, pausing by a stream to drink. I fill my wineskin with water and douse my face as well. I feel dirt and sweat cling to me, and I decide that my first order of business upon clearing the trees is to bathe. For a while, the only sounds that I hear are the chittering of the birds and the scurrying of creatures in the trees. Although the fact remains that I have no idea what will greet me once I am past the gorge, I cannot help but admire the land around me. Moss and ferns drape across rocks and fallen trees; multiple thin streams all run away from me to meet and become Devent Falls. Battlewood is not perfect, but it is beautiful in its own wild way.

I stop to eat a meager meal of dried meat and an apple. I have filled my stomach but the loose feeling from the mead still lingers, and I do not feel completely connected to my body. It is better that I feel this way than to focus on the impending death of my family, though, and I do not stop drinking. I swagger through the forest, singing a ballad about the brave warrior Casden who saved Battlewood from certain destruction. I am louder than I would otherwise be, thanks to the mead. My voice echoes through the sprawl of beech and beech-oak trees. Mosquitos, my only audience, attempt to land on me and leave itchy welts. I swat at them in annoyance.

Before I realize it, I have cleared the mouth of the forest and I am standing at the edge of the gorge. My song cuts short as I take in the scene before me. The grey rocky cliff side is covered with patches of brown and green moss, as well as the occasional tree or group of wildflowers that dare to fight gravity. Nearby, a large wading pool gathers and water falls in a heavy rush, cascading down the side of the cliff. A fallen tree lies across the mouth of the gorge as a makeshift bridge. It will get me into Garyn, if I do not fall off of it first. At the bottom of the gorge, across the river, there is a wooden trail built into the wall. I follow it, trying to find a way to get onto that trail, and find nothing. My only option is to climb down the cliff.

Sighing, I reattach my sepiwin to the strap across my shoulder. This is going to be difficult, and I am regretting that I ever brought the mead with me. My head spins if I look too far down, and I learn quickly to keep my focus in front of me. I fumble and grope around the cliff's wall to find a handhold until I finally find a solid spot in the rock and begin my descent onto the rarely-travelled rock path. I make it roughly halfway down the cliff before the rock changes completely and becomes more fragile and the path narrows. Tentatively, I take my next step. As I let go of the rock above me, pebbles begin to fall, and I realize I have made a mistake. The rock crumbles from beneath me before I can catch my footing.

Letting out a shout, I tumble down the side of the gorge, falling ten feet before I can stabilize. Wrist throbbing, I curse myself for getting drunk. And then, before I can grab hold of the cliff, the rock shelf gives way beneath my feet and I am free-falling toward the water.

...... † ......

When I come to, I am surprisingly dry and comfortable. Immediately, I am aware that I am no longer at the gorge. I sit up quickly and press a hand to my temple as my head swims. It passes after a moment, and I am able to take stock of my surroundings. There is no light, save for a fire crackling in a small stone hearth in front of me. From the ceiling hang ropes of shells, ambers, and stones wrapped in twine. They are mesmerizing as they twist and catch the light from the flames. I reach up to touch one.

"You're awake."

I draw my hand back quickly and whip around, trying to find the source of the voice. Behind me, a figure—a woman, judging by their tone—stands in a doorway, shrouded in shadows. She walks toward me, hands up and open in front of her. "I do not mean to frighten you." Her voice is soft, melodic.

"Who are you?" I ask, watching her through narrow eyes as she comes to stand by me. "What do you want?"

"May I sit next to you? I have to tend your wounds," she says. She holds up a jar and a small cloth.

"I...alright," I say, still watching her closely. In the light, I am able to make out her features. She does not seem to be much different than my own eighteen years of age. There is a stark contrast between her wild, unbound copper curls and my icy silver hair, usually pulled back in braids and a tight ponytail. I get the feeling that there is no force in the world strong enough to tame her hair. When the light catches her eyes, I am able to see that they are hazel and framed by long lashes. They are much warmer than my own, a cool silvery-grey. We are like fire and ice sitting side-by-side.

She uncaps the jar and reaches for a small wooden spoon inside. When she withdraws the spoon, there is a heap of yellow-colored paste on it. I eye it warily. "It's a calendula poultice, to keep infection at bay," she says. "You cut yourself pretty badly when you fell into the water. I was able to take care of most of the wounds, and that broken wrist, but this cut is fighting me." I am suddenly aware that my wrist is pain-free. I examine it, awed.

"What did you do?" I ask, twisting my wrist left and right. It seems to be completely healed. "How did you know that I fell into the water?" Was I being watched? How had I not noticed? Oh, right: the mead. I lecture myself silently about my drinking until she cuts into my thoughts.

"I need your right arm, please." I stick my arm out absently, marveling at my healed wrist again. "I am Willow. I am one of the many healers here." She unwraps bandaging from my forearm and I see a large gash cutting through the cluster of belladonna berries tattooed into my skin. It will leave a scar, and the markings will forever be warped. A sharp pain, one that has nothing to do with my wound, rends through my chest. Of all the tattoos I have, that one is the one that matters most. "You caught your arm on a rough piece of rock," she tells me as she wipes it. "Why belladonna? It is a curious choice. Such a dangerous plant." She spreads some of the poultice across the wound and re-bandages it. I frown and change the subject. I do not share that story with anyone, least of all strangers.

"Why are you helping me?" I ask. "We are enemies."

"Are we?" she asks lightly. She caps the jar and rises. "Get some rest. I'll be back soon to check on you." Before I am able to say another word, she leaves. Huffing in annoyance, I disentangle my legs from the blankets and climb out of the bed. Left with more questions than I have answers, I look around the room. The walls are lined with shelves that hold jar after jar of substances. Along the edge of the hearth, herbs hang upside down, drying. My eyes go back to the hanging ropes, and I reach up. I run my fingers along the smooth edge of the amber and touch the soft feathers and ribbed seashells. They are an interesting combination of things, and I make a note to ask Willow about them when she returns. If she returns.

...... † ......

Willow does indeed return. She is carrying the poultice again, and I stretch my arm out for her. She works silently, and I am the one to break the silence.

"What did you mean, earlier?" I ask, watching her careful movements. She remains silent and I am about to repeat myself when she answers.

"To what are you referring?" She seals the jar, sets it on the table, and looks at me expectantly.

"That we are not enemies," I say. "What did you mean?"

Willow and I stare at each other for a few moments. Finally, she says, "What is your name?"

"You don't like answering questions, do you?" I note. "My name is Jace."

"Garyn has no enemies, Jace. We are a country without war, and thus, without enemies. We are neutral ground. We do not believe that violence solves problems," Willow says.

"But you signed the Pact of Silence," I counter, my brow furrowing in confusion. "Why would you sign the Pact if you are not our enemy?" The Pact, signed nearly one hundred years ago, marked the end of the alliance between the lands. We were taught that an inability to compromise led to a bitter enmity. If what she says is true, however, this does not make sense.

"It was better to enter into a time of silence than into a time of war," she explains. "Every once in a while, your Commander and our Elders will meet to discuss an end to the Pact, but it never comes. Pardon my saying so, but your Commander is resistant to change."

"You're telling me," I mutter. "How did you find me in the water?" I repeat my question from earlier.

"I was scavenging for flora that I need for healing. There are plants that grow only by that bank. I have a feeling that the goddess led me to that spot to find you," Willow says. "Any later, and you may have fallen prey to infection or the elements."

"Oh," I respond lamely. I fiddle with some loose frays on my sleeping dress for a few seconds, trying to figure out what to say next. I am uncomfortable with the idea of magic or gods and goddesses; we have been taught from birth that these are the reasons why we entered into the Pact in the first place. Willow saves me the effort.

"I have brought you clothes to change into," Willow says, handing me a bundle of cloth and leather sandals. "The clothes you were wearing when you fell were ruined. I will wait outside while you change, and then we will dine together."

"Where are my things?" I ask, taking the clothing from her.

"I have other clothing in my pack."

"They are here in this room. Those clothes will not be suitable for this land. They make you look like a warrior."

"That's because I am a warrior," I point out.

"Not while you are in Garyn. Dress," she says, rising. Her long, beaded skirt swishes and clacks as she turns to leave. Sighing, I stand and unfold the clothing she has given me. I shed my sleeping dress and slip into the items. The floor-length skirt, indigo with panels of ivory lace at the bottom, is surprisingly comfortable. I can count on one hand the number of times I have worn a skirt in the past, but I find I enjoy the way the material loosely flows around my legs. I am not so enamored by the shirt: a beige breast band with thin strings instead of shoulder straps. It comes to rest just below my chest, baring the space between the top of my ribcage and my hips. I open my mouth to request a different shirt, but rethink it; I do not want to push their pacifism. Letting out one last sigh, I douse the fire in the hearth and leave the room.

Willow is waiting for me just outside. She examines me for a moment and then nods.

"It will do," she says. "We must figure out something to do with your hair, though." I finger my silver threads self-consciously.

"What's wrong with my hair?" I ask defensively.

"It's very…," she trails off, trying to find the word. "Fierce."

"I am a warrior. That is my job," I remind her. "I cannot

change who I am."

"Nor would I ask it of you, Jace," Willow says calmly. "I only wonder if you might let me re-style it, for the evening." I hesitate and then nod. Willow moves behind me and deftly runs through the long strands, carefully loosening tangles here and there. Her hand softly brushes across the tribal markings etched into the shaven undercut of my hair. "What are these marks?" she asks me.

"They signify who I serve," I say. "Depending on who you serve, who leads you, the marks vary. Those say that I belong to Linota, my leader. Belonged," I amend. I do not belong to anyone anymore. The idea should make me feel free but instead leaves me with a hollowness inside. Willow does not respond, and I feel her pulling and tightening pieces of my hair.

"Finished," she says, coming back around. I feel my hair, and realize she has re-plaited a portion and covered my marks. "We are pacifists, but I cannot pretend your presence will not cause a stir," Willow explains apologetically. "Are you ready?"

"Thanks for the pep talk," I grouse. Willow smiles and then jerks her head.

"This way."

I follow Willow down a short hall, and then we are in a clearing. I look back and see that a narrow canvas tent drapes over what I thought was a hall, and connects to a small hut. The hut is in a circle of similar huts, all of which are centered on a massive, unlit fire pit. All around the pit are stones, herbs, and jars. Beyond the hut, tall fir trees and mossy rocks thicken into a forest, a long wooden trail installed as a path. Garyn's landscape is not much different from Battlewood's, and yet the difference in the atmosphere is staggering. There are no sounds of weapons being forged, no guards patrolling the area, no punishments being handed out. In Battlewood, there are few trades in which the citizens partake, most of them surrounding war, punishment, or defense. If you do not fit neatly into the mold of Battlewood, you struggle deeply. It is the reason why Aleca is facing the fate before her.

I think of my sister, and how she went from a cold prison cell into the wild lands of the courts around us. I wonder where she is, if she is hurt, or even dead. Aleca has always been willful and curious, but impulsive. It is these qualities that have landed her as an outlaw on the run. She has a heart of gold, but no self-control. Despite this, she is my best friend, and I feel her disappearance more strongly than ever. I let out a sigh, and Willow glances at me curiously.

"What is on your mind?" she asks me, tilting her head to the side.

"Nothing, really," I say. I look toward the ground.

"I see," Willow says. We walk the trail in silence, and I take in the scenery around me. There are trees throughout the forest that hang with multi-colored cloths and flags, metal chimes, strings of crystals, and more of the ropes that I saw in

Willow's hut. Runes are carved into trees, high into the reaching boughs, and small glass orbs dangle from the branches. I move closer to inspect the orbs and notice that they are filled with different stones and herbs. The crystals catch the light as it comes through openings in the trees. There is a gentle breeze and the chimes wobble in the air, their songs ringing out. It is a beautiful sight, and I cannot understand why our history books tell us that Garyn is a land of destruction and fighting.

"Has Garyn always been a land of pacifism?" I ask.

"Always," Willow confirms. This only confuses me more, and I am silent again.

Finally, the trail opens into another clearing. This time, it is a circle of small wooden cabins; as with the huts, there is a fire pit in the center of the circle. Unlike the fire pit near the huts, however, this pit is surrounded by stones, feathers, copper dishes, and little multi-colored candles. There is a small fire in the pit, and people sit together in clusters. They are all dressed similarly to Willow: the women wear long, elaborate skirts and cropped shirts, while the men wear loose linen pants with their tunics tucked into a wide leather waistbands.

Willow enters the circle first, and I follow hesitantly. Two men stand by the fire, doling out some sort of stew. Near them, three children stand, waiting for the bowls to be handed to them. They all clamor as they argue over who gets the first bowl, laughing and pushing each other. I survey the rest of the surrounding area, taking in the group of women sitting on the ground in front of a cabin, legs crisscrossed in front of them. They talk amiably as they eat. Willow brings me over to a smaller group of people, and I know instantly they are her family. There are twin children, one boy and one girl, who share her intense copper curls. They appear to be young, perhaps only about four years old. Beside them sits an older woman with sharp, brown eyes and greying auburn hair. She holds light blue and white cords, deftly knotting them together in a row. I watch her hands move with curiosity.

"Mother," Willow greets, waving. The woman looks up from the two children to greet Willow and then freezes at the sight of me. Willow follows her gaze. "This is Jace of Battlewood," Willow informs her mother.

"Well, it is a pleasure to meet you, Jace of Battlewood," she says. If she is surprised or upset, she hides it well. "My name is Acantha, and these are my children, Olea and Persil." Her eyes are wary as she looks me over.

"Hello," I say nervously.

"Why does your hair look like that?" Olea asks, peering up at me. "There is no color."

"Olea!" Willow scolds. "What have I told you about manners?" She turns to me apologetically. "I'm sorry; she has a hard time minding her mouth." Olea has the decency to look ashamed.

"I only meant that it is different," she says, scuffing the dirt ground with a bare toe.

"It's okay," I tell her. "If it makes you feel better, we don't have people with your hair color where I am from. You look different to me, too."

"Really?" she asks, looking back up at me with wide eyes. "Where are you from?"

"Battlewood," I say. "It is just a–,"

"You're from Battlewood?" Persil shouts. The clearing falls silent, and I can tell that everyone is looking in our direction. I feel my face flush, and I turn to face Willow, desperate to get away.

"You should have just left me in your tent. I'm obviously not welcome here. Can I leave now?" I whisper, trying to hide behind Willow.

"No," she says firmly. She places her hand on my back and, with a small push, encourages me to move closer to the fire.

"I honestly should be going," I tell her. "I have…something to do. I have spent too much time in Garyn as it is."

Ignoring me, Willow walks to the men handing out soup and says, "Two, please." They have not moved since Persil's outburst, and at Willow's request, they shake themselves and resume their work. Willow beckons me to the fire pit and sits on a small patterned blanket. Slowly, I walk toward her; I feel the eyes of every citizen on me, and I wish for nothing more than to disappear on the spot.

"Miss," one of the men says, handing me a bowl. He does

not meet my eyes.

"Thank you," I whisper, swallowing hard. I sit beside Willow and mutter again, "Can we please go now?"

"No," she repeats. "We are going to eat and they are going to accept the fact that a citizen of Battlewood is in their land for the first time in a century. It's the shock of it. It will wear off. Now eat. You haven't eaten properly in days."

I am hungry in spite of myself, and I take a bite of the stew. It is free of meat, I assume as a pillar of their pacifism, but still full of flavors and vegetables. A few moments later, Olea settles beside me with her bowl of stew in her lap.

"I am not afraid," she says, sticking her chin out. "And I like your no-color hair. It looks like ice."

"I like it too!" Persil says indignantly, popping out from beside Willow. "Only I was surprised!"

"It looks like you have a couple of ducklings now, miss," the other man says, ladling the stew with a suppressed smile on his face.

Nudging me, Willow nods and points out the others who slowly come to sit with us around the fire.

"Welcome to Garyn, Jace."

THREE

Willow and I walk back through the forest toward her hut. Darkness has begun to settle, and the crystal ropes that caught light earlier are now glowing brightly, guiding us. I stare at them, curious. They remind me of the intricate ropes in Willow's hut. Garyn is eccentric, untamed, and I do not know if I will ever understand anything about it.

"What was your mother doing when we arrived?" I ask.

"Cord magic," Willow tells me. "The colors represent intent. Nine knots bind the intent to bring it to fruition. That particular cord was for wisdom, understanding, and an appeal to the goddess." I furrow my brow as I try to make sense of what she says, but I cannot understand how simple knots would be able to bring any sort of magic about— if magic even exists.

"I see," I say at last, though I do not understand in the least.

"You look pensive," Willow says. "Amber for your thoughts?" She draws a rough piece of amber from her skirts, and I realize that she has sewn pockets into the many folds of fabric. She passes the stone to me, and I take it. I trace the rough edges, examining the translucent honey-orange stone.

"This looks like your hair," I say, holding it near her curls. The moment the words are out of my mouth, I feel like an idiot. She does not seem to mind, though.

"It does, doesn't it?" Willow agrees happily.

"Why do you carry this?" I ask her, still turning it over and over in my fingers.

"It is a stone of healing, as well as protection from negative energies. It cleanses the body of any kind of negativity, and increases luck," she says. "I always carry amber with me."

"You really believe it does all of that?" I ask. I cannot keep skepticism from coloring my voice. There is no way that this tiny piece of amber could do anything more than look pretty on a leather string. "It's just a stone."

"The land is full of energies, of magic," Willow says. "I know that as well as I know my own name." I look again at the small stone in my fingers.

"Well, here," I say, holding it in the palm of my hand. "It's obviously important to you."

"Keep it," she tells me, closing my fingers around the stone. "There are plenty more where that came from. Besides, you seem like you might need a little luck."

I open my mouth to defend myself, but then say, "Considering the circumstances you found me under, I suppose I can't really argue with that. Thanks," I add, running my thumb over the stone again.

"I've been meaning to ask you about that," Willow says. She sticks her hands in her pockets and stares at the sky as we walk. "What happened when you were at the gorge? Why were you there?"

"I fell," I tell her, shrugging. "It was an accident. I guess the rock wasn't as sturdy as I thought it would be, and I lost my footing." I do not answer her other question—I am not sure I am ready to share that piece of information. "Rock climbing was always my weakest point in training. But I thought it would be the easiest way to get across the border."

"It would have been, had you not fallen," she agrees thoughtfully. We drop back into a comfortable silence until we reach the circle of huts. The fire is roaring, and there are people playing music and talking surrounding it. Their instruments are crudely whittled flutes and pipes that play a calm melody. Every few seconds, someone throws something into the flames, and they flare different colors. Willow calls a greeting in a word that I do not understand, and they greet her back with a head bow. I cock my head to the side, watching.

"Why are they bowing to you?" I ask. They have all turned back to what they were doing before. Willow pulls aside a drape of fabric and motions me to walk into the hut ahead of her.

"I am the head healer of Bharasus. We are a small village, but no less in need of a healer than anywhere else," she says as we enter the one-room hut. She lights a fire in the hearth and warmth fills the room. "I was chosen by our Elders two full moons ago." She pulls out the jar of poultice and unwraps the bandaging on my arm. "This is looking much better. You will have a scar, but I can change that, if you want."

"Don't worry about it," I say. "It will be a reminder of humility. I didn't honor the land, and it came back against me." I examine the gash, now a thinning pink line. It tugs parts of the ink on my arm to the side and twists the belladonna out of place. I worked hard to earn my warrior marks, but this is the price I pay for my actions. It is not my first scar, and I know it will not be my last.

"Keep this with you," Willow tells me, setting the jar on top of my packs. "It will stave off infection, should you hurt yourself again. You're planning to leave, aren't you?" she asks suddenly, fixing her gaze on me.

"Yes, I am. I have to. I have to finish what I started." I am not sure how many days I have spent in Garyn, but I know that I need to continue my quest. I do not know where Aleca is, or if she is safe. I cannot handle the idea of my little sister alone in unexplored lands.

A sudden shouting outside of the hut makes me jump, pulling me from my thoughts, but Willow seems unfazed. "Enter," she says calmly. A man, sweaty and breathless, bursts in.

"Healer Finch," he gasps, "it's my wife, she can't breathe!" Willow rises swiftly, gathering a bag from a hook on the wall.

"I will be back in a while," she tells me. "Please do not leave before I return." Turning to the man, she says, "Take me to your wife."

They leave, and I am once again alone in the hut. Sighing, I sit on the floor in front of the fire and pull my packs toward me, relishing the smell of the leather, and the weight of my possessions. I rifle through them quickly, taking stock. Everything that was there before is still there. I root around for a moment and then withdraw the notebook I took from Aleca's bedside table before I left. I open it gingerly to the first page and I am greeted by Aleca's precise handwriting:

This book is the property of Aleca Grimme. Read at your own risk.

I laugh. Aleca often seems much more mature than her fifteen years, but there are moments like this when I am reminded that she is still young. Young, with a death sentence on her head. I sigh and turn the page.

Inside her book, Aleca has fixed a torn piece of paper that shows a map of the courts. The lines on the map form the shape of a nautilus when all is said and done. I trace my finger from the tip of the map, Battlewood, down past Garyn, Kydier, Apaiji, and the surrounding waters and islands. From this page onwards, the notebook is sectioned: one section each for Battlewood, Garyn, Kydier, and Apaiji. Apaiji is circled in red with a star next to it, and I know immediately that this is Aleca's end destination.

The Battlewood pages have the most writing. Aleca obviously has been trying to gather information about all of the courts. There is some information beside Garyn, accompanied by a sketch of the gorge and a sketch of some mountains, but that is all. I pull out a small pot of ink and a metal-tipped pen. Beneath the header of Garyn, it says:

Appears mostly uninhabited. Forests and waters. Saw a white deer. Some brown and speckled birds. More to come as learned.

I dip my pen in the ink and add my scrawling handwriting beneath Aleca's words:

Garyn is a pacifist country. Adheres to Pact of Silence as a means to avoid conflict. Welcoming to those who mean them no harm. Believes in magic?

I pick up the amber that Willow gave me, and examine it. I have a hard time believing that one small stone can provide protection, but Willow seemed adamant in its abilities. I cannot say whether I have been exposed to magic in my life —

Battlewood has strict laws against it and people have lost their lives as punishment for practicing magic. I turn back to the last page about Battlewood and write:

Resistant to change.

I cap the ink, wipe off the pen, and tuck them and the notebook securely into my pack. I will finish what Aleca started. Battlewood will learn.

...... † ......

When I open my eyes, it is morning. As I sit up, a blanket falls off of me. I did not realize I had fallen asleep while I waited for Willow to return. I look around, searching for her, and find no one. I rise stiffly, rolling my neck to stretch it out. Sleeping on a stone-and-wood floor isn't the most comfortable, and my body protests it loudly. As I stretch out the kinks, Willow enters.

"Good morning, Jace." She hands me a small ceramic cup, "Coffee?"

"Is the woman okay?" I ask, taking the cup. I savor the smell of the coffee, inhaling deeply before I take a sip. When I do, it is not bitter, as I expected, but sweet.

"Yes, she's fine," Willow says. "She often suffers from breathing attacks." She turns her back to me and busies herself. I can hear glass clinking, and watch as she selects items and puts them into a bag. I move to the corner where my own bags are, pulling out my standard riding pants and sleeveless tunic. While I am surprisingly sad to have to leave Garyn, I know I have to keep moving. Aleca is out there, and I have to find her.

I quickly pull my pants on under my skirt and slip into my breast band and tunic. I fold the borrowed clothing and set it on the edge of the apothecary table, and then turn back to face Willow. She is still packing her bag, and I clear my throat.

"Willow, I have to be going," I tell her. "I have to do… something, and I cannot put it off any longer."

"I know," she says, not turning around. "If you can give me five more minutes, I will be ready to go."

"You're not coming with me," I say, frowning.

"You don't think I will just let you waltz into unknown territory alone, do you?" She turns and places her hands on her hips. "You need my help."

"I do not need anyone's help," I say. "I have gone on plenty of trips by myself. I know how to keep myself safe."

"Maybe you know how to keep yourself safe in Battlewood," she corrects me, "but you do not know how to keep yourself safe in lands with which you are enemies." Willow crosses the room and rolls onto the tips of her toes, reaching for something on a high shelf above me. "Garyn has no enemies. I can keep you protected in a way you cannot protect yourself. Besides," she adds, suddenly more playful, "who will patch you up the next time you fall?" She flashes a quirked grin at me, nudges me with her arm, and resumes her packing. I make a face at her and she laughs.

"I thought you were the head healer," I say, crossing my

arms. "You should not leave your people in need."

"I already took care of it. Don't bother trying to change my mind. I am coming with you. I will be your ambassador," she says, snapping her bags shut. "I will keep you out of trouble. Get your pack." She reaches up to the ceiling and takes down one of her ropes with stones and feathers.

"You make it seem like I am a barbarian," I grumble. "What is that thing, anyway?"

"A witch's ladder," she tells me, delicately wrapping the rope around her wrist and knotting it in place. "It is used for casting intentions. In this case, it is spelled with requests for protection and guidance from our goddesses. You do not believe in goddesses?" she asks, seeing the look on my face. I shake my head.

"We believe we are ruled by one commander, chosen through a contest of strength," I say. "We do not place stock in magic, gods and goddesses, or the unseen."

"But who do you pray to for harvest, for protection, for mercy?" she asks, brow furrowed. "Where does your spirit reside when it has left this life?"

"It doesn't," I say, shrugging. "Once you're gone, you're gone." Willow shakes her head, and a few errant curls tumble out of her loose bun.

"No goddesses, no magic," she mutters, hitching her pack and walking down the hall. "What a strange land to live in."

I look around her hut, dimly lit by the light streaming

through the windows, and then pull out the amber that Willow gave me, staring at it. "I could say the same thing," I say softly, running my thumb over the surface.

We spend the day preparing. It is the least I can do for Willow, who has appointed herself as my bodyguard and chief liaison officer. I walk her through my standard mode of operation. She is, for her part, a dutiful student. Several times, I have to tell her to pack lighter. She protests each and every item I cast aside, trying to advocate for its need. I cock my head to the side, listening as she makes her passionate plea; when I point out that she will be in charge of carrying all of it on her back and waist, she becomes more amenable to streamlining her belongings.

I try to not to focus on the fact that time is continuing to slip away from us, and that the distance between me and my sister is growing further and further with each second. I would never admit this out loud, but I am grateful that I will not have to make this journey entirely alone. Warriors have lost their minds from isolation in the past and I have no interest in joining their ranks.

At last, the day begins to draw to a close. We make our way to the clearing where we have eaten all of our meals. More people are gathered there than I have seen since my arrival. I did not realize that Bharasus had the capacity for this number; I suppose many of them live tucked away as Willow does. The fire in the center pit is fully stoked and roaring. Beside the flames sit a man and a woman playing music on intricate instruments which I have never seen before. One hand turns the crank at the base of the instrument, while their other hand flies across what looks like a miniature stretch of keys, warping the pitch of the sound that comes out. It sounds like a mixture of a fiddle and an organ, and it is intoxicating.

As the music picks up speed, people begin to dance together around the flames. The faster the music plays, the quicker and more jubilantly they dance. My jaw is hanging open. "This….is incredible," I say, watching the scenes around me.

"This is Bharasus' way of wishing us luck in our journey," Willow tells me. "Whenever one of our number prepares to leave for a period of time, we provide a send-off. The food we will dine on tonight has been magicked with protection. The musicians are playing the songs of our ancestors to remind us that these paths have been walked before."

"And the dances?" I ask.

"To celebrate," Willow says with a shrug. "We encourage adventure and expansion. Would you like to try?"

"I don't dance," I say immediately. I am sturdy on my feet, but useless when it comes to the behaviors and actions that have been coded as a woman's duty. I got that from my mother. My father, always one for breaking those gendered roles, was a beautiful dancer, lithe and graceful. He also knew that if he were to dance with us, he needed to hide the breakables first.

"Nonsense," Willow says. "Everyone dances. Dance with me, and I'll show you."

I continue my remonstration, but it falls on deaf ears. She takes hold of my hand, small and soft; my hands are covered in callouses and scars. Willow tugs me toward the large group of dancers that has formed in the time I've spent trying to weasel out of participation. Grumbling, I allow myself to be pulled. I stand still and watch as Willow releases me and begins to twirl around, curls whipping around her face as she does so. When she realizes I am not moving, she grabs my hand again and forces me to jump around and spin with her. It's impossible not to be drawn into her joy, the music, and the fire. I let myself go and join in the celebrations. We don't stop until the sun begins to peek through the trees.

...... † ......

"This is a lot harder than I gave you credit for," Willow says, hitching her skirts up around her knees as she clambers over rocks and fallen trees. She has tied her curls up in a messy bun, and there is dirt streaked across her face. We pause while she regains her breath, resting with her hands on her knees before straightening up again. We both know we have limited time before the sun begins to set. Willow has already warned me that the land will change quickly and dangerously the closer we get to the border of Garyn and Kydier.

"I did not become a warrior because it would be easy. I like a challenge," I tell her, flashing her a grin. "If this map you made is right–,"

"–Which it is–"

"–then we should make it to a water source in another couple of miles. We can set up camp there and make dinner," I tell her. From where we are, it is difficult to determine how high in the sky the sun is, but I assume that we are nearing its setting. We have been making steady progress across Garyn since we set off this morning, and I can see that Willow is wearing out.

"Why did you become a warrior?" she asks me. We are walking side-by-side again. I have to remind myself to pace myself to meet Willow, and I shorten and slow my steps. Despite our height difference, I can cover ground faster than she can. I shrug, watching my feet as we walk.

"My mother was a warrior, until she hurt herself. And I guess I have always liked the idea of being the one to protect those who are important to me." I do not mention that it was a choice between serving my land or my head on a plaque in Raznik's quarters.

"But that means death, does it not?" Willow asks me.

"What do you mean?" I ask, looking over at her. Her brow is furrowed as she thinks.

"Battlewood spares few people," Willow says. "We know this from history and experience: Garyn has lost people to Battlewood's violence."

"We do what we must to protect," I say carefully. "We do not kill for sport, but sometimes battles do end in death, yes."

"I see," she says. She is silent for several minutes and then asks, "Have you…?"

"I am not proud of it," I say quickly. "But if it comes down to losing one life of a stranger or many lives of friends, family, neighbors…"

"Even though that one you have killed also has loved ones back home?" she counters.

"Our focus is on our own, not the lives of strangers," I say. "What kind of warrior would I be if I risked the lives of those around me by showing mercy to someone who shows no regard for our rules, our land?"

"It would seem we will not find common ground on this," Willow says lightly. Despite her conversational tone, I am aware that this particular discussion has been ended.

We lapse back into a quiet march, broken only by the sounds of cracking twigs and the calls of birds hiding high in the leaves. I chew on my lip nervously. I fear that a rift has formed between Willow and me. What friendship we did have was fragile at best, and I worry that even this has devolved. However, my plan from the start was to make the journey to find Aleca on my own. If Willow decides to turn back, then at least I have made it this far with her assistance and—I hope— am that much closer to my sister.

We make it to the mouth of the forest and are greeted by a bubbling creek. We dip our cups into the water and drink greedily. The water is like ice despite the heat of the day, and it is all I can do to stop myself from submerging my head in it. As Willow unpacks items to cook dinner, I pull out our bedrolls and the large canvas tent we brought from Bharasus.

I have set up the tent and lay out my bedroll beside the fire. She watches me, confused.

"What are you doing?" Willow asks. "I brought the tent to protect us from the elements, our bedrolls should be inside it. Why are you looking at me like that?"

"I didn't want to assume you would be happy sharing your tent," I say. "When we were training to become warriors, we were taught to fend for ourselves. I thought perhaps you would want to do the same." I think about the awkward silence after our argument. I cannot nail down whether she is bothered by my presence or not. Our differences are so great.

"Just because we do not agree on everything does not mean we can't share a tent," she tells me with a little laugh. "A difference of opinion is bound to happen eventually."

"It just seemed like a big thing to disagree on. I worried that it upset you," I say. "If you look in the front pocket of my bag, you'll find some cloth balls. Grab two, and add some water. They are for soup. No meat," I add. as she opens her mouth.

"Thank you," she says, smiling again. I make a noncommittal sound and return to setting up camp. get to work on the tent. Annoyed with myself for getting worked up, I kick the tent spikes into the ground. It is out of character for me to behave like this.

I join Willow at the campfire and hungrily tuck into my soup. I slow down halfway through, savoring the warmth of the vegetables and broth.

"Try this," she says, handing me a slice of something pale green that feels dry but soft to my touch. I eye it, unsure.

"What is it?" I ask, sniffing it suspiciously. She gives me an encouraging nod, and I take a tiny bite. It is sweeter than I expected it to be.

"I thought you might like it," Willow says with a laugh as I greedily finish her offering. "It is a pear, one of my favorite fruits."

"I wish Battlewood would trade with Garyn again," I sigh as I reach for another piece. "We are really missing out." Willow laughs again. She is good company and I cannot understand what led to the Pact of Silence all of those years ago. It is something the last few generations have been born into and taught to accept blindly. Sharing an affable meal with a Garynite is an unheard of concept in Battlewood, and yet Garyn has proven my own court wrong time and again.

"What do you know about the other lands?" I reach behind me and extract Aleca's notebook from my bag.

"I know plenty," Willow asks, startled. "Why?"

"I am sure you have figured out by now that I am not out here for leisure," I say. Willow nods slowly, watching me rifle through the pages. "I am trying to find someone, and fast. They were trying to learn about the lands, and got…interrupted. I want to finish this for them."

"May I see it?" she asks. I hesitate and then hand the notebook to Willow. She opens it and begins to read. "Aleca Grimme…" she murmurs. "Your family?"

"My little sister," I say, swallowing hard. "I have to find her, Willow."

after the last fall

FOUR

She moves in a circle, speaking in a language that I cannot understand. The witch's ladder is wrapped tightly around her right arm. I watch intently as she works, curiosity overcoming my distaste for magic. When she is finally finished, she returns to join me by the fire.

"What did you say?" I ask, motioning at the invisible circle.

"I asked for protection, and for guidance from my guides," Willow says. "When one accepts the beginning of their training, they are chosen by three guides. It is these guides who cut and shape the path I will take on my life journey."

"What if you've been given a life journey that you don't want?" I ask quietly, pulling my knees up and wrapping my arms tightly around them. I can feel her looking at me, but I stare resolutely at the ground.

After a moment's silence, Willow says, "Then you must find a way to challenge and to change." There is a long pause, and then she asks tentatively, "Does this have anything to do with your sister?"

I open my mouth to answer, and then close it again. How can I tell Willow that my life journey is to find my sister and drag her home to her death? How can I challenge this journey without bringing death to Aleca or to us both?

"I think I'm going to turn in," I tell her, brushing the dirt off of my pants as I stand. "Wake me if you need anything." With that, I cross our site and enter into the tent where our rolls have been laid out.

I cannot understand how Willow can stand to be near me. We are the antithesis of one another. I should tell her the truth. I should tell her that we are not on a rescue mission, but fulfilling a death sentence. Instead, coward that I am, I slip into my bedroll and nestle myself into a cocoon of blankets, grateful to be inside the tent. Soon after, Willow enters as well. I hear her whisper my name, testing to see if I am awake. When I do not answer, she sighs and quietly lies beside me. Her breathing soon mellows into an even hum, and I mimic the rhythm to lull myself to sleep.

······ † ······

Sleep, when it comes, does not come easily. I am falling, falling, and then come to a hard stop on a cold floor. Valkyrie Elouned stalks around me, eyeing me like a captor watching its prey. I am paralyzed as she darts toward me and then quickly retreats, taunting, and laughing callously. From everywhere and nowhere, Raznik's voice booms out, "Bring them in!" Doors screech open and a line of three people come staggering in;

they are bound to one another by chains. I recognize the icy silver hair of my mother and sister, the salt-and-pepper hair of my father. They are blindfolded as they are dragged to the center to stand before me. I want to reach out to touch my parents—it's been so long since I've seen them—but do not. Valkyrie Elouned surges toward me again.

"Get up," she commands me. I am no longer paralyzed, and I rise with the shakiness of a newborn colt. I do not move fast enough for her, and she grabs me by my hair to a standing position. I let out a sharp shout of pain.

"Jace?" Aleca says, looking around wildly. "Jace, is that you?"

"It's me, Al," I confirm, voice shaking.

"Jace, what's going on?" Aleca asks me. "I'm scared."

"Me, too," I whisper. I force myself to look up into Valkyrie Elouned's eyes. She stands a full foot above me and cuts an imposing figure. She is draped in her execution garb, and my blood runs cold. From behind her steel-feathered mask, her gold-and-crimson flecked eyes glint with a cold humor.

"You know why you are here," she tells me. "Take a good look at your family, for it shall be your last."

"No!" I shout, shaking my head. I try to step backward and she throws a wing out to stop me.

"This is your life journey," she tells me, handing me her execution blade. "Kill them all." She pushes me forward. "Kill them, or I will do it for you."

"I can't," I whisper. " Kill me instead. Leave my family alone."

"Is this your choice?" she asks me. I nod silently, and she takes the blade from me. I close my eyes, prepared for the cold cut of metal on my skin. When it does not come, I open my eyes, confused. I see her raise the blade, and then swiftly brings it down on Aleca. She does not have time to scream before she is motionless on the ground. Twice more, I'm forced to watch as Valkyrie Elouned murders my entire family before me. I scream and cannot stop myself. I shake where I stand, my vision swarming.

"Jace!" Raznik calls out. And then it becomes a softer voice, sweeter. "Jace!" the new voice cries. I shake one last time, and suddenly I am no longer in the chamber of Battlewood, but rather in a tangle of blankets in a darkened tent. My face is slick with tears and my throat is sore.

"Jace," the voice says again, and I realize it is Willow. The tent is lit by a candle, and I see Willow staring concernedly into my eyes, her hands on my shoulders. "Are you alright? You were screaming like...like..." Words fail her and she shakes her head.

"I'm sorry. I'm okay. Go back to sleep," I tell her hoarsely. "I free myself from the blankets as quickly as I can and leave the tent, embarrassed to be seen this way. I wipe at my eyes and clear my throat as best I can. What I cannot clear is the sight of my family lying dead before me. I stifle a sob as I crouch at the bank of the creek; I scoop a few handfuls of water to my face, trying to cool it from the hot tears.

"You cannot get rid of me so easily," Willow says mildly as she sits beside me. I hadn't heard her approach. I hide my face from her and watch the water as it lazily gurgles down its path. I wipe my cheek off on my shoulder as a couple of errant tears escape. "Do you always have to be so strong?" she asks me. I clear my throat again and turn to look at her.

"I'm a warrior, Willow," I tell her. "I have to be strong. Emotions can be used against you, weaken you. In battle, emotions can mean your demise."

"We aren't in a battle right now," she tells me, touching my arm lightly. "It's just you, me, and the creek."

"I know," I whisper, fearful my voice will crack.

"What were you dreaming about?" Willow asks me curiously. "You seem to have nightmares often. You had them when you were healing, too, though I suspect you don't remember much of that time."

"I…my family," I say. I watch my reflection in the water as I speak. My pale face is distorted by the bubbles and ripples, like looking into a shattered mirror. "Always my family." My voice catches in my throat again. Shake it off, Grimme! It was just a dream, I tell myself. But it seemed so real. The hot blood of my family spilling onto the stone floor, glinting like rubies in the firelight; the cold metal in my sweating palm…I cannot shake the memories.

"We will find your sister," Willow says firmly. "I promise."

"I know we will," I say.

I do not tell her that's what I'm afraid of.

...... † ......

We are fighting again. We have managed to make it three more days without incident, swapping stories of our childhoods, of the differences in our courts, of little things here and there. But no matter how light the conversation between us is, it always ends up coming back to the one glaring difference between us: pacifist versus fighter. Neither of us can come to a compromise on the matter without completely disowning our own selves in the process, and it remains a bitter thorn in our sides.

"I don't understand you," Willow says, climbing over the tumbled rocks and fallen tree trunks. It is one of the last obstacles we face before leaving Garyn behind and entering into lands which neither of us knows. From here, there is a wide body of water to cross; on a raft or boat is the only way to enter into Kydier from this part of Garyn. I see Willow stumble as she clears the largest of the rocks and I immediately reach out, grabbing her arm to stabilize her before she can fall. "You do things like this," she says, motioning at my hand still fixed on her arm, "but then have no problem taking the life of another for indiscretions."

"I never said I didn't have a problem with it," I say, casting Willow's arm away in disgust. "You did."

"Well if you don't like it, then why do you do it?" she challenges. I glance over at her and see her staring at me with a mixture of frustration and confusion. The sunlight catches her eyes, turning them into an almost iridescent hazel.

"Why do you care so much?" I volley back. "It's not like you'll even see me again after we've found Aleca, so why do you keep pushing this?"

"Why won't I see you again?" she asks me, tipping her head to the side. Her voice softens.

"What place does a trained killer have in a pacifist healer's life?" I hear the bitterness in my own voice.

"The place I've made for you," Willow replies. I am taken aback by her statement and do not know how to respond. Instead, I turn away from her. She does not say anything more, but I feel her close behind me. Several times, I move to speak and then change my mind. I cannot see how either of us will ever be able to overcome this thing that divides us. Its presence is constant and looms over us at all times, the unspoken truth that keeps us at arm's length.

If I'm being honest, there is a part of me that is expecting Willow to come to her senses and realize that she does not want to be with me. I wonder if she thinks that I may turn on her someday. She puts on a good front, but I've seen the way she looks at my clothes and my weapons, the tattoos that crawl up my arms, around my neck, and down my back. I am a constant walking reminder of the lives I have had to take. Everything that Willow is, I am not. I cannot understand how someone so kind, compassionate, and warm, has teamed up with someone so cold, reserved, and jaded. The two of us together, in any capacity, makes no sense—even if I want us to.

We prepare dinner together, working side by side but not speaking. We sit across from one another to eat, the flames of the fire casting shadows across our faces. It isn't until I've finished my meal and reach for my pack that Willow breaks the silence.

"Tell me something about yourself," Willow says as she peels the skin from a fruit. I do not speak until I've finished emptying my bag.

"What do you want to know?" I ask, tipping my bag upside down; I give it a hard shake and bits of herbs, stones, and twigs tumble out.

"What do you want me to know?" she counters, handing me a piece of her fruit. "Peace offering," she adds with a smile. I wipe my hands on my pants and take it. My knee-jerk reaction is to say nothing, but Willow's unabashed interest gleams in her eyes, and I sigh.

"I don't know what to tell you. Ask me a question and maybe I'll answer it," I say. I watch her as she chews thoughtfully. This is a fine line to walk, and I wait nervously.

"If all contact with outside courts has been cut off, why does your commander insist on an army?" Willow asks me.

"For security," I tell her. "We still have people who try to infiltrate our lands. And we have people who leave our lands. Raznik believes they are threats to our land and our safety. He fears an overthrow of our government."

"That's why Aleca fled?"

"That," I decide to trust Willow with the truth, "and the fact that she has been practicing magic. There is no higher treason to our land."

"What does Raznik hold against magic?" She is trying her hardest to understand the laws of my land. The more time I spend trying to understand, though, I find the less I do.

"I…don't know," I finally say with a shake of my head. "Raznik fears being overthrown. I don't know what our land was like before the Raznik dynasty took over, but I know that the bloodshed and destruction from that takeover was unimaginable. Since then, it has been a rigid land with no room for error. The slightest misstep would find you hanging by your ankles in the dungeons." I pause before adding, "I'm lucky that I was given another chance."

Willow is quiet again, and I let out a sigh of relief. The questioning was not as difficult as I expected. I've sighed too soon, though, for Willow begins her line of fire again.

"What were you like as a child? Did you always want to be a warrior? Do your parents mind that you became one?" The questions tumble uncontrollably from Willow's lips. I hold my palms up to stop her.

"I said one question, not a whole interrogation!"

"I want to know," she insists.

"Okay. Let me think. I guess I was an alright child. I was

adventurous, but never a rule breaker. Not at first, at least. That all changed when I was fourteen."

"Why?"

Another follow-up question. Of course.

"My dad died when I was eleven, and it was just me and mom raising Aleca. But then my mom died three years later, in a battle. I don't think my parents would be surprised that I became a warrior. Mom was one, too."

Willow hands me another slice of fruit. "Is that why you started breaking rules? Because you were left alone to raise your sister? Why didn't any adults help?" She's obviously been waiting for a chance to quiz me and I realize that I am not going to get out of this. I have to indulge her.

"That's how it is in Battlewood. Our neighbor helped when she could, but I was old enough to cook, clean, watch after Aleca...that's just how it works," I say. "But I guess the trouble started when I fell in with the wrong people."

"Tell me about them," Willow encourages. "There isn't much opportunity for trouble in Garyn. We find the honor system is effective— when you're not being oppressed, there is nothing to rally against."

"There's not much to tell," I say. "I met Tally on the night of my mother's funeral, and we continued hanging out, even after–," I cut off, nervous to continue.

"After?" Willow encourages gently. "You can tell me."

"Even after I was imprisoned. The only reason I even got

out was because of Raznik. Which is ironic given that he's the one who sent me on this mission. Drinking, drugs, going across the border in the dark," I answer before she can ask why I was arrested. "Tally and I were chaos together. I knew I was an idiot, and I knew I was going off the deep end, but there was just something…I don't know, addictive about her."

"What do you mean?"

I pause, thinking about Tally's wolfish grin, her black hair curling in tendrils down her back, her bright blue eyes. I think about the way her voice would get husky when she was pitching her newest scheme, the way she would wind her hair around her finger, the way she would pout until she got what she wanted.

"Like…like you only ever cared about impressing her. We did a lot of stupid things together, but they never felt stupid in the moment. Tally could make anything seem like the next great adventure, and after fourteen years of following rules and doing as I was told…I don't know, I guess it just caught up with me. There aren't many people I'll let get close to me, but Tally managed."

"Are you and Tally still friends?"

I swallow hard before I respond. "No, uh, she…she died. About a year ago now. That's when I sort of turned myself around, until all of this stuff with Aleca started."

"What happened?" she asks with a soft gasp. Her eyes are wide and misty.

"Have you ever heard of flying ointment?" When she shakes her head, I explain, "It's some old folklore from before anything remotely related to magic was banned from Battlewood. It was said to help witches fly. It's all nonsense, but it does make you hallucinate. Anyway, Tally found her great-great aunt's recipe and tried to make it, but…I don't know, she misread the recipe, or ignored the warning. Either way, she used too much and the belladonna poisoned her. I told her she was stupid to try it, but she wouldn't listen."

"The belladonna tattoo is for her," Willow says, gently touching my scarred forearm. I nod.

"That was Tally, though. Once she got an idea in her head, there was no changing her mind." I smile sadly. I can still feel the chasm that Tally left in my life. "Well, I think I've said enough for the night. You're too easy to talk to."

"You were in love with her," Willow says. It is not a question.

I hesitate for a moment, ready to deny it. Willow's voice is tender, though, that I instead admit the truth, "Yeah, I was. But it doesn't matter now, so…" I trail off and busy myself with repacking my bag. The day is finally beginning to catch up with me, and my emotions are raw and fried from oversharing. I wasn't planning on telling any of that to Willow, and now I feel like an insect on display.

"Of course it matters. Love always matters," Her hand covers mine as she speaks.

"We have an early start tomorrow. We should turn in," I say, rising and giving Willow a feeble smile. I enter the tent and, without undressing, I wrap myself in blankets and fall asleep to the ghost of Tally's laugh in my mind.

...... † ......

We trudge across the tumbled rocks that begin to turn into shale and sand. A small port has been built at the mouth of the sea. There is a single small rowboat bobbing on the water. There is no one around to lay claim to the boat, and Willow sets her sights on it. As the shale continues to give way to sand, I notice assorted shells and little bits of stone heavily peppering the shoreline. I stoop to examine them and see that they are smaller pieces of the same roughly-shaped amber that Willow gave me. Absentmindedly, I bring a hand to touch my own amber, wrapped in a leather thong and tied around my neck for safekeeping. I scoop a small handful of the shells, amber, and sand and dump it into an empty tin in my bag. I cannot explain the motivation behind this, except to show Aleca, or maybe to serve as a reminder of my time in Garyn. Straightening up, I look over and see Willow untying the boat from the dock. She has already placed her belongings inside and is ready to cross the waters. With a slow exhale, I make my way over to the boat.

"Are we allowed to take this?" I ask, crossing my arms. I don't need more transgressions in my ledger.

"Of course," Willow says. "These boats are here for those who need them. Honor system," she explains. I fight the urge to roll my eyes. Of course they work on the honor system. Instead, I nod.

"Do we know what we are getting ourselves into?" I ask, glancing out at the expanse of the water. From the shore, you cannot see the next piece of land. I have no doubt that this is going to go poorly, the two of us alone in a tiny rowboat, making our way across unknown waters, into unknown lands. I know that Willow trusts the energies of the earth to carry us along, but I do not always have this same faith.

"We will be fine," Willow says confidently. "Kydier has never been on poor terms with Garyn. And these waters are filled with protectors. If we respect them, they will respect us. Are you coming, or not?" She seats herself and stares up at me expectantly.

"Against my better judgment," I mutter, swinging a leg over the side of the boat. With a grunt of effort, I cast us off, and then we are alone except for the sea.

...... † ......

We are halfway across the water when we spot them. At first, I think that it is an illusion, an effect of the sun's blinding reflection on the water. However, as Willow points them out, I realize that we cannot possibly be suffering from the same illusion. I squint, trying to better discern what we are seeing. From where we float, I can make out vividly-colored masses. They do not appear to be moving, though it is difficult to tell. I would prefer to continue moving past them, but Willow insists that we try to get closer. After a brief debate, I find myself rowing the boat closer toward the colors.

Pinks, greens, blues, and golds begin to become clearer as we approach, and I realize that we are looking at some sort of otherworldly creature.

"Sirens," Willow whispers. I make a face as I think, trying to remember what sirens are, but cannot recall. "Sea creatures. Women who lure sailors to their death with their song. It's all an illusion of lust and beauty. I've never seen one in person before! Get closer," she says, still whispering. "Can you hear that?"

"Willow, this isn't–,"

"Just a bit. We won't bother them, I promise," she says. Her eyes are pleading, and I grit my teeth. Damn her.

"Fine. Just a bit," I repeat emphatically. I row slowly, and the faint sounds of a song begin to fill my ears. It is both melancholic and triumphant, and I strain to hear more. With more gusto, I row closer. The creatures—the sirens—are coming into clearer focus now, and I can see that the brightly-colored masses are their hair. There are six of them total, all female. They all wear their long hair adorned with various stones and shells; it pools and floats around them as it reaches the water. Excluding their hair decorations, they are completely naked, and I can feel my face turning pink. Despite my shock, I am eager to get closer to them, as close as I can. All of Willow's warnings are driven from my mind as I take the sirens in.

The song grows stronger, and I feel drunk with the music. The closest one, the one with shimmering golden hair, moves close to my side of the boat. She is clearly the leader of the women, and she sings only to me. Strings of pearls twist through her hair, and she hands one of them to me. I reach for them and our hands touch. In the background, I can make out the supporting songs of the others, and it is maddeningly wondrous in its allure. I can feel myself standing, ready to leap from the boat and follow her intoxicating song for as long as I can. I have never seen a woman so beautiful, so seductive and enticing. I want—no, I need—to get closer, to be with her. Gripping tightly to the pearls, I lean over the edge of the small boat; she smiles as she places a hand on my arm, and then my face. Her touch leaves a trail of faint golden dust. I watch it catch the sunlight, enthralled by the promise of it.

I swing a leg over the edge of the boat, reveling in the warmth of the water and the beauty of her song. She puts her hand into mine and then I am in the water, floating alongside them. The linen of my clothing flows around me in the current, and I feel weightless. Her song picks up pace and the other women come to join us.

"Stay with us," they say. Even their speaking voices are like the most beautiful melody. The golden girl wraps her arms around me, stroking my hair and tracing her fingers down my cheek. I know I will agree to anything she asks of me. One by one, the women begin their descent back under the water. The golden girl laces her fingers into mine and then dives down, disappearing beneath the water. I follow suit, kicking my legs to keep up with her. The water turns from a clear turquoise to a deeper indigo. The temperature changes and a chill takes over my body. I feel a firm pressure wrap around my ribcage and I am rising toward the surface again. I reach a hand out toward the mysterious golden woman but she disappears.

I fall back into the boat, hitting my shoulder hard on the looped metal that holds an oar in place. Pain brings clarity back to me, and my vision is filled with Willow's face, concerned and angry. I shake my head, trying to clear my mind. Water drips down my forehead and into my eyes. I brush away the hair that has plastered itself to my face. The song has stopped, and I hear an angry chattering.

"Sireive, nonaris!" Willow shouts. A horrible shriek sounds, and the boat is rocked by a wave. When the water settles, it is silent again.

Shakily, I ask, "What was…what happened?"

"She was prepared to lure you away and take you as a lover," Willow says. "It would appear that you were ready to accept her offer," she adds shrewdly. My face burns. An illusion of lust and beauty, that was what Willow told me. An illusion I fell for in an instant.

"Why did you have to go after them in the first place, huh?" I ask, anger masking my embarrassment. "'We won't bother them, I promise!' Hah!" I let out a derisive snort. I am still mortified by how I allowed myself to be lured so close to the depths. I realize I am still clutching onto the pearls, and I throw them into the water. They float for a moment, and then slowly sink into the water in a spiral. I watch them for as long as I can, reluctant to look at Willow. Finally, I ask, "What did you say to her?"

"Siren, she is not yours," Willow says. "She was most displeased. I'm sure you felt her departure." I nod, rubbing my shoulder as I think. "I'm sorry I hurt you, but I had to bring you back."

I wave a noncommittal hand. "Why didn't she affect you?" I ask. My face is still warm, but the worst of it has receded.

"I'm not sure," Willow says. "My guess is that you enticed her in a way I didn't. Perhaps my magic protects me. Or perhaps it is because I have devoted my energies to protecting you; my desire to keep you alive outweighs any other desire." She says this so matter-of-factly that I am forced to look at her. Her face is serious, with no hint of humor. We stare at each other for a long moment, and then move in unison to each take an oar. Whatever that moment meant, it has passed, and we are back to business once more.

"Next time," I tell her, "I'm calling the shots."

...... † ......

I am growing uneasy as we near the shore. Nighttime is settling in, and I do not want to set foot on foreign ground in the black of night. In a coup, it is desirable; in an attempt to remain as unseen as possible, not so desirable. Willow, as usual, is optimistic about our circumstances. I have to take a few seconds before responding. Keeping my annoyance in check is never something that I have particularly excelled at, but I do not want to lash out at her. I don't understand how one person can be so unrelentingly optimistic about everything. She could find the silver lining even if my hands were wrapped around her throat. Indeed, even now, she is rowing the oars steadily, her eye trained on the shoreline of Kydier. I cannot make out much beyond a clear line of trees. The shore of the water slowly tapers back into a narrow estuary that runs between the trees and disappears. Shrouded in the darkness, it makes for an imposing silhouette, and I am hesitant to near it.

"Willow, I think we should wait until morning to enter," I say cautiously. "I've been on the planning end of night-time invasion too many times to pretend that this looks innocent."

I can see her trying to think this through. "I don't know what is in these waters," she says slowly, bringing her hand to her mouth. She nibbles the nails of her right hand—I've noticed that she seems to do this often when she is deep in thought. "There are creatures here that are more than meets the eye." I know she is thinking about the sirens again, and I turn pink.

The same thought has crossed my mind, and I cannot decide which side of me is going to win out: the reluctance to face magic, or the reluctance to look like an enemy intruding. Finally, I say, "I think we are at a greater risk if we enter into a stranger's land without thought. If someone were to enter into Battlewood in the night…"

"They would be killed," Willow finishes.

"At the very least, they would be chained and taken for prisoner," I say. I stare out across the water, trying to see any sign of life. I see nothing and turn back to look at Willow. "We stay on the water, and enter at first light," she agrees.

"Get some rest; I'll keep watch," I offer. She awkwardly pulls her long legs straight out in front of her and uses one of the benches as a makeshift bed and her pack as a pillow.

"Good night, Jace." She is silent and then adds quietly, "I'm sorry about the sirens." She avoids my gaze, turning onto her side.

"Good night, Willow." She says nothing else, and I sigh, stretching out my legs and trying to find a comfortable position. My eyes scan the shore, and across the sea. For a second, I think I see something—or possibly someone— luminescent and blue darting across the surface of the water. Before I can focus my gaze, though, it is gone and there is nothing. And then I see it again, further off, but there. It runs on the tips of its toes for a moment before disappearing. As it appears a third time, it has brought company: one the same color as the first, and another that is the color of green seafoam. I pull out Aleca's notebook, trying to sketch them as best as possible given the lack of light and the darkness of my charcoal. I have managed a smudgy likeness of the creatures, and make a note to ask about them in the morning, when Willow has woken. Her breathing has already evened out, and I am grateful for an excuse to remain awake: if I do not sleep, I will not dream.

······ † ······

I watch the sky as the sun slowly creeps upward. There is a terrible beauty in it, and I feel nearly overwhelmed by the sight of it all; melancholy, nostalgia, and awe all fight to take center stage in my mind as I drink in the swirls of pinks, purples, and pale blues. The water reflects the myriad of colors and the whole scene glows as the sun gains strength. I gently shake Willow, whispering, "Wake up. You have to see this." She makes a sound halfway between annoyance and acceptance and sits up stiffly.

"See what?" her voice is hoarse from sleep. She rubs her eyes, yawning like a puppy, and I am shocked by the sudden realization that I have developed a soft spot for her. I can count on one hand the number of people in my life for whom I have cared, and they are all Grimmes. Grimmes and now one Finch. Maybe I've been away from Battlewood too long. Or maybe Willow's influence is changing the way I look at things. I know I am not the same as when I left Battlewood three weeks ago, and I know it is by Willow's hand. Challenge and change.

"The sunrise," I motion to the sky around us. Her eyes widen as she observes the canvas of pastels, and I hear her gasp quietly.

"It's..." Her words fail her.

"I know." As she watches the sky, I root around in my bags, looking for something to eat. We are low on supplies, and I am hoping that we can replenish in Kydier. I manage to find some dried fruits and jerky, and hand the fruit to Willow. We sit in a comfortable silence, watching the sky shift from pastel purple into a strong, bright blue. Finally, we pick up our oars and begin to row toward the shore of Kydier.

We row slowly into the river, taking in the scene around us. A pale green light filters through the trees, casting an odd glow over our skin. The sea branches off in two different directions. As we move further inland, the water begins to move more swiftly, and I can hear the sound of a drop-off ahead. We've taken the wrong route. Willow realizes this at the same time, and we scramble to paddle backward.

It becomes evident quickly that we are making no progress, and I see Willow's eyes widen with panic. We are getting closer to where the water falls, and have a short window of time to get out before we go over the edge. As fast as I am able, I shove all of our belongings into our bags.

"Can you swim?" I shout to Willow.

"Yes."

I grab the bags, and throw them as hard as I can. They barely make it onto the land but thankfully catch on a flat rock that juts out into the water, and rest there. Some of our things will be wet, but it is better than losing them altogether. "Get ready to jump!" I call. There is no time to give more directions. We both stand and the boat begins to tip. "Now!" Twice, the water washes over my head, and I kick to the surface spluttering. Willow is nearly to the rock, but I can see her losing strength. I kick as hard as I can, my shoulders shrieking as I thrash through the wild waters, desperate to reach her.

I manage to grab her and spit out a mouthful of water to shout, "Swim for me! We're almost there." Using the last of her energy, and with my arm holding tightly around her waist, we push against the intense current together. I feel her muscles tighten as she propels herself with my help. She is little more than dead weight and I clench my teeth harder as I pull through the intense current. The water makes my eyes sting from the grit and debris but I can see we are nearly there.

We make it to dry ground and turn to see the boat wobble at the edge of the fall and then drops. Doubled over with my hands on my knees, I pant,

"Well, that's one way to get there. Battlewood owes you a rowboat." There is a moment's pause and then we both break down with laughter. It is a hysterical laughter, the kind that arises out of a giddy relief, and we are powerless to stop it. I drop to the ground, and we lay on our backs, chests heaving with. We eventually calm ourselves enough to sit up straight and take stock of our surroundings. We are both a mess; the dirt and debris on the ground has turned to mud in our wet hair, and our clothes are plastered with mud as well. With no option to wash up, I pull a string of leather from my bag and tie my hair into a bun. As Willow busies herself with her bags, I quickly strip down to my breast band and undercloth, kneel at the edge of the water, and wring out my clothing.

There is no chance that I will be able to wear them for a while, and I root through my bag to find a fresh pair of leather pants and a sleeveless tunic. The weather has turned humid and heavy, and I find myself longing for the cool caves of Battlewood. I dress hurriedly. I do not know where the citizens of Kydier reside, and I would rather my first interactions with them be while I am fully clothed. I turn to speak to Willow and see her standing with her back to me, completely unclothed. A strangled noise rises from my throat and I whip back around quickly. I don't know what to do with myself, and I stare adamantly at the water until Willow speaks.

"Are we ready?"

I chance a glance over my shoulder and see that she is fully clothed again.

"I-mhm," I say. "Ready."

······ † ······

The trees form a horseshoe-shaped basin around the waterfall, and a well-carved trail has been formed in the sides of the cliffs, down into Kydier. We gingerly step onto the first step, testing its threshold. It appears strong, and we make our way down slowly.

"I saw something last night," I tell Willow, "out on the water.

Have you ever heard of a creature that runs on water and glows?" I feel foolish as the words leave my mouth.

"Something that runs on water and glows?" she repeats. I see her thinking for a moment. "My guess would be sprites."

"Sprites?"

"Spirits that inhabit a certain space. Sprites, nymphs, sirens, they're all similar. Garyn has many tree sprites and wood nymphs, if you know how to approach them."

"I didn't see anything like that in Garyn."

"Well, you weren't exactly welcoming to them, were you?" she asks loftily. "They know when they're wanted."

"No, I guess not," I admit. As we scale the path, I am able to look around. The land appears similar to that of Garyn, with the obvious exception of the heat. It is beautiful, with the bright greenery and blue waters. Across the way, I can see the ruins of what was once a temple built into the rock wall. It is mossy and abandoned now, but looks as if it was wondrous in its time. There are more ruins peppered throughout the area and I point them out to Willow.

"Kydier is a land that also believes in gods and goddesses. It makes sense that there would be temples here," she explains.

I do not understand the concept of praying to gods and goddesses. Everything we have in Battlewood, we have created. We build our own walls, toil our own soil, and farm our own goods. Our hands create it all. We are at the mercy of the elements, not at the mercy of some other beings. I voice none of this, though. There are several topics that Willow and I disagree upon, and this is one of them. I concede that there are creatures in the world that defy common nature—I have seen them for myself. But that is just it—I have seen it. I have never once seen proof of a god, or a goddess. Perhaps if I did, I would change my mind.

Lost in my own thoughts, I do not realize we have come to the bottom of the path until I move to take another step down and lurch forward instead. We are at the foot of the waterfall, which feeds into a large swimming hole and trickles away in a small stream. The broken wood of the rowboat bobs in the wake of the water, stuck against a boulder. It is an impressive sight to see, and I watch the cascade of the water for a few seconds before looking for our best path. Now that we have made it down the wall, the land is far more open and easier to look across.

The ground becomes paved with broken up bricks and stones. More ruins rise up, powerful and imposing. It is evident that they are still visited daily by people, despite the fact that they are falling down. Many of the ruins, pillars and broken statues, are decorated by intricate mosaic inlays. I wonder briefly if this is where Battlewood got the idea to create a mosaic coat-of-arms. Battlewood and Kydier were once trading partners, after all.

We forge ahead steadily, looking for someone, anyone, to speak with. It is high afternoon before we finally come across another person, a child. She cannot be more than six years old, and she stares at us with wary, deep brown eyes. She is dressed in a bright flowing frock that deepens the russet color of her skin. I nudge Willow to speak—I am terrible with children. I cannot begin to imagine what this child was doing by herself, so far away from anyone else. But then again, children are taught to wield a knife at her age in Battlewood, so I guess I cannot speak to Kydier's practices.

She speaks to the child in a language that I do not understand. I hear our names, but nothing else means anything to me. I watch in awe— what other talents and abilities have I yet to learn about Willow? She kneels to match the height of the girl. "What's your name?" She asks this question in the common language, a test to see if the child can speak with both of us.

The girl simply continues to stare at us, curiosity and fear in her eyes. I am about to tell Willow to give it up when the girl whispers, "Ela."

"Ela, we are not from Kydier, and we need some help. Do you think you could help us find an adult?" Willow asks, this time in our language. She smiles cheerfully at the child. Ela nods, and begins to walk. Willow rises and exchanges a glance with me. I raise an eyebrow— we're to follow this child? With a shrug, Willow begins to follow the little girl as she leads us down the brick path and into a village. There are people milling about; they, too, are clad in brightly colored fabrics but do not all share the same brown skin as Ela. They talk animatedly with one another, until we are noticed.

Our appearance has an immediate effect. As we enter behind Ela, silence falls. A man close to Willow snatches Ela up in his arms and speaks to her in the same language that Willow used. I cannot understand what he is saying, but the message is clear from his tone: we are dangerous. Willow raises her hands, to show that we mean no harm. I stuff my hands in my pockets, feeling uncomfortable. This is the second time my presence has caused a stir. I could not look more different from these people, with my icy hair and pale skin, and it is clear that I am the outsider, the root of the discomfort.

"What do you want?" the man holding Ela asks. His voice is thick with an accent; this is not his native tongue.

"We're trying to get to Apaiji," I say, trying to keep my tone even and welcoming. His dark eyes flick to me for a moment and then back to Willow. "You do the talking, Willow," I mutter.

"We mean nothing but peace," Willow says gently, "and we ask for nothing but perhaps a meal and a place to rest. We have been away from our homes for some time."

The man confers with several villagers for a moment, speaking in their rich foreign tongue quickly and quietly. Finally, a woman comes forward. Her eyes are kind, though I can see clearly that she is uneasy.

"Village Yolchame can offer you these things which you ask," she says. "But you will please leave your weapons outside the village." I open my mouth to disagree—do none of these courts want to protect themselves?— but Willow quickly cuts me off.

"Thank you," she says. I nod my thanks, chewing on the inside of my lip to keep from arguing. I am reluctant to be without my blade when I know nothing about these people. However, I do as they ask and let them watch as I remove the sepiwin from the strap on my back, as well as a small knife from inside my bag. Slowly, I set them in a basket and cover it with a piece of dyed wool they have provided. This seems to appease the villagers, and they slowly return to their conversations, but I see their furtive glances as we pass by.

One man in particular catches my attention, and the hairs on my neck rise at the sight of him. He is young, but older than either of us. He does not appear to share many traits with the rest of the villagers; his skin is only a shade darker than Willow, and his facial features are much sharper. He could easily be from Garyn or Battlewood, and I wonder briefly if he is native to Kydier. His eyes, cold and calculating, watch Willow closely as she walks by, and I see him brazenly scan her body. He sucks his teeth at her, and I ball my hands into fists at my sides. I do not trust him. I have seen what eyes that cold can do, and I make a note to keep alert around him. As we pass, he reaches out and grabs her wrist. She stops to stare first at her wrist, then at him.

"If you decide you'd like some different company, come find me," he purrs in a husky voice. Unlike his peers, his voice is just barely tinged with an accent. "Just ask for Bamet." Bold as you please, he lifts her hand to his lips and kisses it.

"I'm quite comfortable with my company, but thank you anyway, Bamet," Willow says as she slides her hand out of his. Her tone is even despite the steeliness in her eyes. I have never seen that look before, and it's nice to know that she has the capacity to feel anger. Perhaps she is not so relentlessly optimistic as I'd come to believe. I flash a small, triumphant smirk at him as we pass. His face darkens with displeasure, but he says nothing more. The woman, and the man carrying Ela, step forward to us.

"Follow me," the man says. "I am Romek. This is my wife, Klara. You have met our daughter." We fall in behind the family as they guide us through the village. Most of the houses look the same. They all connect to one another and are made out of a pale clay-and-stone mixture. All of them rise up and taper off, giving them the appearance of a line of beehives. Various tools, pots, ropes, and vases clutter around the outside walls. In the center of the village, there is a large stone fountain of water.

We pass by some tall poles with long, heavy strings connected between them. Clothes hang from them, drying in the hot sun. I think of the grimy items in my bag and wonder if I could wash them here. Maybe I'll have Willow ask.

Romek and Klara stop at the end of the row of houses. Romek holds out his hand, motioning for Willow and I to enter into their home. It is more spacious than it appears from the outside and divided into two bedrooms, a kitchen, and a common space. The walls are hung with intricate tapestries that mimic the appearance of the mosaics which I've come to understand as the calling card of Kydier. Copper and pewter pots and pans pile on top of the hearth in the kitchen, and there are brightly-painted dishes precariously stacked alongside. The common space is filled with mismatched cushions and pillows, all centered on an elaborate pipe with two hoses connected, one on either side. Klara leads us into the smaller of the two bedrooms, where a single bed mat is laid out.

"Ela will sleep with us tonight," Klara says. She scrutinizes me for a moment, and I smile nervously. "I do not mean to stare," she says apologetically, "but you look very much like another girl who came through here some time before you. She called herself…" She trails off, trying to remember.

"Aleca," I supply in a half-whisper.

Aleca was here.

after the last fall

FIVE

We have been given the chance to recuperate alone. I do not think I am even fully prone before I have fallen asleep. Despite my unease in this village, despite the knowledge that Aleca has come and gone through this same place, I have been awake for almost two days straight, and it has caught up with me. When I awaken, it is dusk. The sun is setting and the sky is ripped with deep golden-red and blue. The scent of cooking food wafts through the air, and my stomach grumbles loudly. I rise and tentatively step into the common space, where Willow sits with Ela. They are playing together with a faceless doll wearing a dress similar to the one Ela has on. Willow looks up, smiles widely, and goes back to playing. I return the smile a moment too late, and then turn my attention to the kitchen, where Klara is standing at the hearth.

"You will help, please," she says, jerking her head for me to come join her. I do so, and she places a wide terracotta bowl in my hands. It is filled with chopped vegetables and a multitude of something small and white. I examine it for a moment.

"What is this?" I ask.

Klara glances over at the bowl as she stirs something in a pot suspended over the flames. "Rice," she tells me. "A filling food. We eat much rice in times of hunger. A little bit fills you for a long time." She goes back to stirring whatever liquid is in the pot, and then adds, "Hold the bowl steady, please. Romek usually helps me, but he is at a village commune right now."

Dutifully, I tighten my grip on the bowl, and she adds in a large ladleful of broth. I am amazed that she can stand to be in front of such a hot fire when it is already so hot outside. Even in my thinnest clothing, I can feel the fabric clinging to my body with sweat.

"What is a commune for?" I ask. She takes the bowl from me and places it on a short table beside her. Placing an identical bowl of vegetables in my hands, she begins the process again.

"To discuss change," she says. "You have much change ahead of you," she tells me suddenly. "You must learn to be less like stone, and more like water. Too much hardness will be your downfall. You know the other girl who came through here? She is much more like water."

"Aleca is my little sister," I tell her. "When was she here? Was she okay? Did she say anything?"

"Your sister was fine," Klara says, taking the second bowl from me. She motions to the painted dishes and I grab a stack of them. "She was here two weeks ago, but did not stay more than a night."

Mind racing, I ask,

"What do you mean, be more like water?"

"You have a hard path to take," Klara says calmly. "You have difficult decisions. Stone can change, but only under great pressure. Water is always moving, always changing, always moving forward. Do not let yourself crack. You must allow yourself the chance to soften. You have already felt yourself changing: grow through the changes; grow with them." She places a gentle hand on my cheek, and it is so motherly that it brings tears to my eyes. I have not realized how much I miss my parents until this moment. "Gentle, forward movement," she murmurs. Without another word, she picks up the tray on which the bowls of soup are balanced and brings them outside. Ela is quick to follow, and Willow joins me at my side.

"Are you okay?" she asks me, touching my arm softly.

"I will be."

...... † ......

We have all gathered to eat outdoors on a huge rug. It is woven with strands of turquoise, gold, and brown; the main focal piece of the rug is a massive tree in the center. I run my fingers along the design, mesmerized.

"Our gathering place," Klara tells me. "We eat as one village together." She motions toward a group of men and women who are walking together. "See them come from the commune?" The people stare at Willow and me as they draw closer, and I have the distinct feeling that we were the topic of discussion at the commune. Despite the stares and curious glances, we are met with no hostility. Everyone comes to the rug and sits in a circle, centered on the tree. Romek stands in the middle of the circle and raises his hands. Around him, the people of the village hold hands with one another and raise their arms as well. Shyly, Ela slips her hand into mine. Willow takes hold of my other hand; I glance quickly at it, and then at her. She stares straight ahead at Romek, the left corner of her mouth upturned slightly. I press my lips together tightly to keep my face straight and turn my gaze to Romek.

"We ask for blessings for this food. We thank our guardians that we may come together yet another day. We ask that we maintain the protection of our guardians as they deem fit, and pray that we grow through change and understanding. As it will be!"

"As it will be!" the villagers chant back. Willow and I say it a moment later than the rest but are awarded a nod from Romek regardless.

"We welcome our new visitors, Jace of Battlewood, and Willow of Garyn. I hope you will all extend hospitality to them as you would anyone else. Let us eat," Romek finishes, taking a seat beside Klara. The bowls of rice and stew are passed around, as well as a large pot of ground meat mixed with onions, spices, and bread crumbs. Drinks are poured, sweets are handed out, and everyone begins to eat. It is evident that meals are prepared and provided by several villagers, and I wonder if it is always the same people, or if it changes. Willow politely declines the dish of meat, and a man sitting near her challenges her.

"It goes against our way of life to eat meat," she explains. "Please, do not be offended. I mean no harm."

"Then what is your way of life?" a woman across the circle asks.

"Well, we believe in pacifism," Willow says. "Cause no harm, lest it come back to you. We do not fight, we do not injure or kill. Even the smallest life is still a life."

"And does Battlewood share this same thought?" the woman asks. It is all I can do to keep from laughing out loud.

"No," I say. "We believe…" I trail off, trying to word our beliefs in a way that does not make us seem cruel. "We believe that poor behavior merits consequence," I finally say. It's not a lie, but not quite the truth either. Battlewood's unofficial motto is: Kill first, ask questions later. There is no way to keep ourselves from sounding cruel; until this moment, I've never stopped to think on it. Even more surprising, I feel discomforted by it. Before, I followed blindly, did as I was instructed, and accepted it as our way of life. But now…now, it seems foolhardy, archaic, and cruel.

"It is curious that you can live so near and be so different," Romek comments.

"Battlewood and Garyn do not speak," Willow says.

"Battlewood does not speak with anyone outside of our land," I state. "Not since the Pact."

"It appears they do now," Klara says, smiling. There is a knowing look in her eyes, as if she knows what Willow and I have gone through together over these past few weeks. Willow and I look at one another and smile as well.

"Yes, I suppose they do," Willow agrees.

······ † ······

"Jace?" comes a whisper through the darkness. Willow and I lay side-by-side in the small room laid out for us. Kydier rises and rests with the sun, and have requested that we do the same while we are guests. We have agreed to do so. However, as both Willow and I are used to resting much later into the night, we both lay on our backs, eyes open and staring at the ceiling.

"Yes?" I whisper back.

"I was just wondering if you were awake," she says. Silence follows, and I turn my head on the pillow to look at her. I cannot see much beyond her outline, but I feel her turn to look at me as well. Here and there, I catch a glint of her eyes.

"You know what Klara said earlier, about how our lands talk now?" I ask. "I thought you should know that…that not everyone in Battlewood agrees with the Pact of Silence, especially people our age, or younger. We don't all want to be enemies."

Willow is so still and silent that I worry she has fallen asleep, but then she says, "That is good to know. Thank you." I make a non-committal sound in my throat and turn my head back to look at the ceiling again. "Jace?" she asks again. I turn to face her once more.

"Yeah?"

She says nothing, but laces her fingers in mine and rests her head on my shoulder. I do my best to keep my breathing steady, but I know she can feel that my heartbeat has sped up. I trace circles on her palm, and we lay silently together for a time.

"Good night, Jace," she eventually whispers, pressing herself closer to me. Her breathing evens quickly, and I know she has fallen asleep.

"Good night, Willow," I whisper, smiling softly as I close my eyes.

······ † ······

The first thing I see when my eyes open again is a pair of bright brown eyes and two tufts of hair tugged into pigtails looming just above my face.

"Up!" Ela cries, taking my face in her hands. She squeezes my cheeks together and laughs at my puckered lips. She does the same to Willow, who, for all her pacifism and general love of the world, does not wake with grace.

"What are y-oh, good morning, Ela," Willow quickly corrects.

"Breakfast is ready, come eat!" she says as she runs outside.

"You thought it was me, didn't you?" I ask, amused. Willow

runs her fingers through her hair sheepishly. "You don't do well with the morning, huh?" I rise and twist my hair into a bun. As I run a hand across my scalp, I realize that my warrior marks have grown in and are no longer there. It's just one more reminder that I am no longer who I was.

"I do fine with mornings," Willow sniffs. I raise an eyebrow at her, and she amends, "Well, I could if I had to." I laugh and pull her into a standing position. Her hand lingers in mine for just a moment before I pull away and turn to walk outside. I wonder if she is thinking about last night too. Willing myself not to blush, I join Klara, Romek, and Ela outside. Willow and I seat ourselves beside Klara, who hands us each a bowl of breakfast. I see our clothing hanging to dry above the fountain; someone took it upon themselves to wash it for us.

"No meat for you, Willow," Klara says, "but meat for you, Jace. Eat—it will strengthen you." I sniff my food carefully as I bring a forkful to my mouth. It smells full of spices, and I take a bite. Immediately, my eyes water as heat floods my mouth.

"It's delicious," I croak. Romek hides a smile behind his hand, and Klara hands me a piece of pink-colored dried fruit.

"Eat this to cut the spice," she tells me. "Kydier makes food differently from Battlewood?" I think on the spices and meats we eat—flavorful, but incredibly mild.

"Very," I say. I nibble at the fruit, and it does cut the heat in my mouth. "What is this?" I ask, staring at it.

"Apricot," Romek says. "Our land's fruit."

"Well, thank you," I say, "I think the fire may eventually die out." I take another bite, savoring the sweetness. There is still some jerky in my packs—I'll eat that for breakfast later.

...... † ......

After our meal, Willow excuses herself to investigate the surrounding trees; she says something about there being different herbs or flora of some kind. I am not sure exactly what she is looking for, but I assume it's for her tinctures and poultices. I decline her invitation to go with her—I spotted a waterfall earlier and am longing to get the grit out of my hair and from underneath my fingernails. I intend to take full advantage of the fact that I have had a full night of sleep and am more alert than I have been in some time. I try to get Willow to agree to carry something sharp on her in case anything happens, but she refuses. After a short argument, we part ways and I stomp toward the water with a huff.

I have just finished washing the soap out of my hair when I hear a scream. My eyes snap open and look around wildly, searching for Willow. She screams again, and I scramble to the shore, where my clothes sit. Without thought, I pull my dry breeches and tunic on over my soaked undergarments; I can feel my bare, wet, feet squelching inside of my boots as I run toward her. I stumble as I race and let out a stream of curses. Wiping my hands on my legs, I realize that I am without a weapon; another stream of curses tumbles out of my mouth. I am a fool for not following my own advice to Willow. Finally, I burst through the foliage and find Willow pinned against the trunk of a large, twisted tree. A man, wiry but strong, has his hand around her throat, and she struggles to loosen his fingers. Discarded wildflowers and herbs lay at her feet.

As I get closer, I see that he has his face nestled into her neck, just below her ear. My heart drops through my stomach as I realize what he intends to do to her. Her eyes are wide, scared, but she does not attempt to harm him. I take a few steps closer, searching around for a way to distract him, or a way to arm myself—whichever comes first. I pick up the largest, sharpest piece of rock that I can find, feeling its heft in my hand. It will serve either purpose. I hear him mutter something to her, and only then do I know who her captor is.

"Bamet!" I shout, leaping down the sloped land. "Willow, fight back!" He whips his head around, grins, and tightens his grip. I can hear Willow's breath, ragged and harsh. She will not fight him, even if it means her own death. Whether she remains still due to pacifism or an inability to defend herself is neither here nor there—she is helpless either way. "Damn Garyn," I mutter through my teeth. I readjust my grip on the rock, gripping it so tightly that I feel it pierce my skin. "Leave her alone!"

"Just giving the lady what we both want," he says with another cold grin. He turns his focus back to Willow, who has clenched her eyes shut. As quickly and as silently as I can, I cross over to him. By the time he notices me, the sharpest point of the rock is pressed against the side of his neck.

"Where I come from, we kill rapists on the spot. Let her go," I growl. Bamet releases Willow to swing at me. His fist catches first the corner of my eye and then my jawline; stars burst into my vision. As I fall, I catch the side of my face on a branch and can feel it rip open my cheek. Taking advantage of my temporary blindness, Bamet turns his attention back to Willow, pulling greedily at her clothing. The stars clear. Able to see again, I leap up and, in one swift move, bury the tip of the stone deep in his neck. He falls, and Willow drops with him. She rises shakily, and I turn my back on the slain man. "Let's go," I say, climbing back up the slope toward the waterfall where my pack is.

We walk back toward the waterfall silently and quickly. I can feel Willow watching me, and I turn to face her. Her eyes linger with disgust on the blood spattered across my face like crimson freckles. Anger and disappointment rise in my throat and fight for dominance. My head throbs from Bamet's fist, and I cannot keep the edge out of my voice.

"Say it," I challenge her, stepping forward. "I know you've thought it the whole time. I want to hear you say it. I want to hear you say that if you were in my position and the roles were reversed, you wouldn't kill to save someone you…someone you…" I cannot say it. Instead, I let my words fade away. By this point, we stand almost nose-to-nose. Willow is silent as she stares at me. I shake my head with a humorless laugh and turn away, wiping the blood off of my face with my arm. This is what I get for allowing any space for emotion or feeling. She remains quiet as I shove my belongings in my pack and sling it across my back. "Thank you for getting me into Kydier. I'll be fine now. Tell Romek and Klara that I'm sorry I couldn't say goodbye." Without another word, I start forward without her.

As I leave, I drop the leather thong that carried my piece of amber. It falls to the ground with a muffled thud, and I am gone.

...... † ......

By the time I've stopped to rest, there are several miles between us. I cannot tell where I am; all I know is that I am following the stream. Water always leads to a source. I seat myself against a tree. It is only now that I allow myself to cry. In a way, I knew it was only a matter of time until something like this happened and I am angry for setting myself up this way. I opened up and let someone in. I allowed myself to care—no matter how much I pretended otherwise—and I've been left the fool for it.

I take a shuddering breath and pull out Aleca's book. Its pages are filled now with my messy scrawl and Willow's curly script. I stare at her writing angrily, half-tempted to draw thick lines through her words. Knowing how it would pain Aleca, though, I refrain. Instead, I examine the map Willow drew for us.

The lands form a sort of nautilus when all is said and done, land and water merging to connect. I draw a line from the topmost land, Battlewood, and drag it in the spiral down through Garyn, into Kydier and then the center of it all, Apaiji. I do not understand why the lands all spiral out and around Apaiji, but I am certain that this is where I will find Aleca. If Apaiji is anything like the rest of the land around it, it will have all kinds of magic, creatures, superstitions—all of the things that Battlewood denounces. And, if I know Aleca, that is the exact reason why she will have gone there.

Even as a child, I can remember finding Aleca huddled beneath a blanket with a lantern, scribbling wildly as she wrote her magic stories. I can remember hearing our mother and father whispering when they thought we were asleep, worrying over what they would do with her. They never had a concern with me; there was never any doubt that I would follow in my mother's footsteps and become a warrior. I played dress-up in her armor before I could even speak a complete sentence. But Aleca never showed a care for the ways of Battlewood. Aleca has always had her head in the clouds. For a while, I was able to keep her feet on the ground, even if her head was in the clouds. But over time, that became harder and harder to do, and she started floating further and further away.

When our father died, Mother and I shared the burden of caring for Aleca, who was only seven. Although I was eleven years old, I was already headstrong and stepped into the role of my father with ease. When our mother died in battle three years later, Aleca became my responsibility, and I took it seriously. There were times when I was unreachable, however, and I know that it was in those moments that she began to follow her interests in earnest. I knew there was no hope of trying to shape her into a warrior, like my mother and me. Instead, I tried to train her in the arts, in literature, and in history. Nothing worked; Aleca could not be deterred from pursuing her research about the outside lands. It did not help that I became a stranger to her, lost to my own vices and whims. Tally and I became inseparable, which furthered the distance between Aleca and me. I stopped paying attention to her almost entirely. When she was discovered, she was taken into solitary imprisonment, deep in the reaches of Battlewood Castle. She was only a child at the time; as her failed guardian, I was kept separated in a different cell.

Every day, Raznik came by, tried to beat me into submission, into giving up my sister. He also saw personally to Aleca's torture. We were eventually released, with the promise that there would be no more border crossing. Of course, that didn't last. When he realized he could not break the Grimme sisters, he called for a hearing to determine Aleca's fate. It was all for show—he intended to kill her from the start. I know that Raznik has commanded me to bring my sister back as a means to eradicate both of us at once. He thinks I will not succeed, and if I do not follow his command, it means we both are to die. He gets what he wants regardless of whose hand brings Aleca's death.

I snap the book of notes shut angrily and toss it to the ground beside me. I have never realized how suffocating silence is until now, without Willow to cut through the quiet. Nothing is the same as it was before, and I cannot tell who is to blame for that: Raznik, or Willow. If Raznik had not sent me on this mission, I would not have met Willow. But, if I had not met Willow, I would not have begun to question my lands. I would not have begun to build relationships with other lands. But, most of all, I would not be so unbearably alone right now.

...... † ......

A night and another half day pass before I stumble across a pop-up marketplace. I assume this means that I am near either to another village, or to Apaiji itself. I do not have much money with me, but I have brought some. Whether Battlewood's currency is accepted here is another matter entirely. There are stalls lining the sides of the roads and people shouting out their wares and goods. Quickly, I sort through my money. I need food, certainly, but I also am without a weapon. Food, I can find in nature, but I want a manmade weapon by my side

I move between the carts aimlessly, looking over all of the different items for sale. It appears to be an eclectic mix of wares, ranging from clothing and home goods, to stones, bottles, and items I cannot even identify. Among the stones, I spot amber, and my stomach drops. I look away quickly, and continue my search for a weapon. Finally, toward the end of the row of carts, I spot a tent with the word 'Blacksmith' burnt into a piece of wood. I duck under the flap of the opening and step inside.

A man sits by himself, cleaning a long blade that is lying across his lap. He looks up and locks eyes with me. All that I can see of his face is his eyes, dark but lively. The rest of his face has been covered by a wide strip of cloth. He does not greet me, and I peer around curiously. There is an assortment of weapons in here. I spot throwing blades, glaives, bows and arrows, and nine-section whips. Immediately, though, I am drawn to a dagger, a blade curved like a talon that fits into an intricate wrought-iron handle. I touch it gently, letting out a whistle of appreciation. Whoever has created this is an artist. The man continues to watch me, and I motion to the blade.

"How much?" I ask. He cocks his head to the side.

"Zeim?" he asks. He does not speak the same language as I do. I think for a moment and then pull out a handful of coins. I point first to the coins, and then to the dagger. He picks up a coin and scrutinizes it. His eyes widen and he looks at me again. "Battlewood?" he asks. I nod slowly. He leaves the tent and comes back a moment later with a woman in tow. I swear I have seen her before, but that's not possible—I have never been to Kydier before. She has hard eyes and weathered russet skin; those eyes stare at me with a look of mistrust. She crosses her arms defiantly.

"What do you want?" she asks. Her voice, low and smoky,

has the same hard quality as the rest of her.

"I just wanted to purchase this dagger," I explain. I attempt to keep my voice pleasant, as I have heard Willow do. "I didn't see a cost…"

"We do not need your blood money," she spits at me.

"I don't have much to trade, but I am willing. I am entirely unarmed and have quite a bit of land to cover," I say. I don't know how Willow manages to keep such an even tone at all times; this woman is already testing my limits. They continue to stare at me and I let out a harsh sigh. "Look, are you going to make a trade with me or not?" I ask. She speaks in a hushed tone to the man, her words quick and indistinguishable. They both point to the tattoos on my arms.

Finally, the woman says, "We will trade you the dagger, but only for your hair."

My hand flies to my hair, protective. "My hair?" I ask. "But I…" They know I'm a warrior. That is the only reason they have asked for my hair. A warrior's hair is everything: the marks shaved into it denote the troop, and as you climb the ranks, a braid is added for each rank. I only have two braids, but they have not come without hard work. Even though my marks have faded out as my hair has grown, the braids remain. The man quirks his eyebrow and the woman sets her jaw as they stare at me, waiting.

"What is your decision?" she asks me. I hesitate. The dagger is a necessity, but the cut hair is a means to denigrate me. We both win, in a way, but at what cost? With a sigh, I concede and nod my head. They both smile triumphantly, and the man beckons me forward. "Sit," the woman says, pointing at the stool where the man was seated.

"Wait," I say, holding up a hand. "I'm not letting you both stand behind me with anything sharp. I want you to hold a mirror in front of me so I can see," I tell the woman. "Take it or leave it."

"Fine," she snaps. She leaves the tent and storms back in with an ornately-framed hand mirror. "Your majesty," she says with a mock-bow. We glare at each other as I seat myself. I hear the man rustling behind me and then watch in the glass as he loosens my hair from its tight tail. It falls down in a curtain of silvery-white, and I can feel him running his hands over the strands covetously.

"Just do it," I say through gritted teeth. The woman nods at him, and after a moment, I can hear the sound of a blade shearing through my hair. I let out an involuntary gasp as I watch the strands spiral to the ground.

When it is finished, I stare at myself in the mirror. All things considered, the man could have been much crueler in the cut. Though relatively shapeless, it now falls to rest at my jaw, instead of to the middle of my back. I hardly recognize my reflection. My face has sharper angles and has browned under the sun. It casts an even deeper contrast to the silver of my eyes and hair, and I look altogether otherworldly. I look away quickly and rise.

"Thank you for the trade," I say quietly. "I'll be taking my dagger, now." Gingerly, I pick up the weapon, slide it into its sheath, and attach it to my boot.

"You are playing a dangerous game, ice-girl!" the woman calls after me as I leave. I whip the flap of the tent shut, and do not respond.

…… † ……

I manage to find some rations to tide me over until I get to Apaiji. For all of the welcoming hospitality shown to me by Romek and Klara, there is none of that here. It is exacerbated by the lack of Willow's diplomacy; I am left to fumble through my words and hope that I am not insulting the people around me. I have the distinct impression that I am not doing well with this.

I have set my tent up in the trees, hidden away from the kiosks and other tents. It is against my better judgment, but I feel exhaustion taking its hold over me. I will leave first thing in the morning, before the sun has even risen. I sleep with my hand gripped tightly around the dagger; I refuse to be caught off-guard in the middle of the night. I leave my boots on as well, ready to run if the need arises. I am taking no chances here. I am well aware that I am not wanted in this land.

I cannot fall asleep. I hear the sounds of the merchants as they gather around their fires, talking and laughing. There is nothing here to distract me from the sound of my blood pulsing in my head, from the thoughts intruding where they aren't welcome, or from the raucous bonfires nearby. Annoyed, I roll over onto my side. I stare straight ahead, willing for sleep to come, but it doesn't. I am exhausted, but my nerves are making me a livewire. Some warrior.

Eventually, I drift off into a restless sleep, punctured only by nightmares of hazel eyes and blood.

Crickets are still chirping as I pack up my campsite the next morning. I cannot tell what time it is, but judging by the stars still hanging in the sky, I have not slept long. I will have to stop for rest again later, though I will not do so until I am far from this place. Out of habit, I move to tie my hair back. My hands come away empty, and I remember my trade. Damn this land. I sigh and begin to walk.

I am aided only by the warped and wrinkled map that Willow has created. There are minute tears in the paper from constant folding and refolding, and I move it gingerly as I try to make sense of it. If I am reading it correctly, I am on the outskirts of a small village, then coming up against yet another body of water which, this time, I will have to navigate alone. Just once, it would be nice if I could find two courts connected by a nice stretch of stone and dirt instead of an expanse of water. If I never set foot in a rowboat again, it will be too soon.

The heat climbs as I trek toward the village outlined on the map. Willow has scribbled the name Caroleam with a question mark next to it. It is further than either of us has ever been, and the details of the map become scarcer from this point forward. I keep the map accessible and press on.

Half of the day is gone by the time I arrive at the village. It is the most advanced village I have seen since leaving Battlewood. The places I went through on my way here were developed, but suited to a life without extravagances. I have not seen a true and proper building in more days than I can remember.

The first thing that I notice is a cat pacing back and forth between the two pillars of the wooden entry gate. The creature, black, white, and fluffy, does not pause as I draw nearer. I approach the cat hesitantly; I get the feeling that this cat is the guard of the village, even though the idea of a cat guarding an entire village is laughable. Only when I stop in front of the gateway does the cat turn to look at me. Its eyes are a brilliant gold and I drop to my knees in front of it. I imagine that I can feel my mind being searched and just as a pressure begins to descend into my chest, the cat looks away. I feel a momentary surge of lightheadedness and then I rise back to my feet. The cat moves to one side and I can swear that it motions its head for me to pass.

I feel I should say something as I pass. What does one say to a cat that may or may not be the guardian of a village with questionable ties to magic? I manage a mixture of a grunt and a nod as I pass, unsure of what the protocol is. The city that sits before me is small, but well-developed. It is nothing like

Battlewood, Garyn, or Kydier. I can only assume that this means that I am continuing to draw nearer to Apaiji. There are more apparent signs of magic here, the least of which being the odd cat at the gate. I walk forward several more feet before coming to a stop again. I'm not sure where to turn. There are several storefronts and places that boast ales and food. Further up the road, I spot a sign with the words, "Belladonna Inn," painted in bright golden tones. I snort humorlessly at the name. Desperation wins out over distaste, though, and I make my way to the inn.

It is comfortable inside: the interior is lined with a rich, warm-colored timber. A counter is pushed against a set of stairs, where a man with hair dyed the color of a sapphire sits, bent over parchment. There are mismatched pieces of furniture surrounding a large table where a mixture of people are gathered, talking, and drinking what I assume are coffees and teas. The inn is filled with a smell that reminds me vaguely of the spice cakes my father used to make for us on holidays. I relish the scent of them—I have never managed to recreate his recipe. Taking a deep breath, I walk over to the man with blue hair.

"Excuse me, how do I reserve a room for the evening?" I ask. He looks at me and looks at me quizzically. I know I must look like a mess. My short hair is spiky from wind and lack of sleep, and my boots are caked with dried mud. There are rips in my clothing. At best, I look like a beggar. I pull out what small amount of coins I have left and hold them out for him to see. He plucks one of the golden coins and two of the bronze ones out from the small pile, examining them.

"Battlewood, eh?" he asks me. His voice is deeper than I expected from his waifish body. I nod slightly, unsure of what is running through his head. "Hmm," he says, dropping my money into an intricately inlaid box. "Follow me." I let out a whoosh of breath that I did not realize I was holding and follow him up the staircase. "We have one room left," he tells me. "Baths are drawn for you at sundown, but I will request one be drawn for you now." I flush; it is the politest way possible he could tell me that I look horrible. "You are free to come and go. Will you be needing anything else?"

"Just the room and the bath," I tell him. "Thank you." He hands me a brass key and points to a room at the end of the hall.

"Someone will be by shortly," he tells me before heading back down the stairs. I enter my room and have barely taken stock of my surroundings when there is a knock at my door. I open it to reveal a woman with a stack of towels and a basin full of steaming water.

The moment she leaves, I rush to the basin. It is all I can do not to dump the water over me. I have missed the feeling of warm water and soap. It turns a murky brown as I wash. Bits of grit and debris fall to the ground as I shake out my hair. Once I have finished bathing, I dig through my bag for the last pieces of clothing I have that are in decent shape. Scrubbing the dirt from my boots, I lace them back up and rise again. It is miraculous, what a decent bath can do.

I exit the inn and wander the village, taking in all of the sights. A brilliant white building draws my attention. Where the other buildings are all interconnected, this one stands alone. I make my way toward it, marveling at the way the glass mosaics catch the sunlight and throw it back to the ground. The light creates a multi-colored reflection on the ground in front of the stairs. I stare up at the building slack-jawed. I have never seen anything like it.

"Beautiful, isn't it?" a voice asks. I startle and look over to find a tall man standing next to me. I didn't even hear him approach. I am losing my touch as a warrior.

"What is it?" I ask him. Despite the fact that this man is a total stranger, I feel oddly comfortable in his presence.

"The Temple of the Gods," he tells me. "Built hundreds of years ago, and doesn't look over a day old."

"How is that possible?" I ask, trying to keep the disbelief out of my voice. I am working very hard to understand this new life, and that means that I must accept that things are true whether I like it or not.

"Anything built by the Gods and Goddesses is untouchable," he tells me.

"May I go in?" I ask. He grins at me and gestures for me to move forward.

"Go and see," he tells me. Suddenly nervous, I walk up the stairs. As I reach for the doors, they open on their own. I gasp and jump backward. No one stands in the doorway and I know that my jaw has dropped once more. There is no way they opened on their own…is there? I glance back over my shoulder at the man who I was speaking with, and he gestures encouragingly. I turn back to face the temple and take in a deep breath. A smoky smell of vanilla and balsam fills my nostrils. The source of it becomes apparent immediately: small, stained-glass cones hang from the ceiling, smoke furling out of them that loiters in the rafters.

I spin in slow circles as I observe the temple. It is relatively minimalistic inside. Cushions are scattered on the floor surrounding a massive fire pit in the center of the room. Bowls of herbs and flowers encircle the pit, serving as what I assume to be offerings to each particular deity. I wonder how people learn which deity is the one that means something to them and feel a slight pang of jealousy that I do not have a particular leaning of my own. This, coupled with the way that Willow spoke so reverently of her goddesses, and the statues carved into the cliffsides of Kydier, make me long for something— though I cannot say exactly what it is.

I walk around the circle of the hearth, peering into each bowl of offerings as I do so. An intensely-purple flower catches my eye and I kneel on the cushion before that bowl. I cannot say what it is about this flower, but I cannot move beyond it. I reach into the bowl, take a flower out, and cast it into the fire. The flames roar as they burn a dazzling purple, the same purple as the flower, and I stare, mesmerized. Heat washes over me as the temple goes dark around the fire. A tongue of fire whips out and spirals around me, but the burning never comes. When the flames recede, I examine my hands and arms, looking for burns. Instead, I find a new tattoo, delicate and beautiful, inked onto my thumb. It is the same as the purple flower I was drawn to only moments before. I barely have time to wonder at its significance when a musical, feminine voice whispers into my ear, "You have been chosen, Karishua's Daughter."

SIX

I burst out of the temple, a ball of giddy emotions. My legs
shake like a newborn calf as they carry me back down the
stairs. The man from before is still standing there, lounging on
an overturned produce crate and smoking a long, thin cigarette.
He looks up at me and his face breaks into a sly smile.

"Ah, I know that look," he tells me. "Was someone chosen?"

"How did you know?" I ask. Is that high, breathy noise my
voice? He lets out a laugh and stubs the cigarette out on the
side of the box.

"We have all been there, love," he tells me.

"Please explain it to me. Who chose you? What does it
mean? Is everyone chosen by someone?" I remind myself of
Aleca as the questions tumble out, one after another. I cannot
stymie them though.

"Come with me," he says, casting an arm around my
shoulder. "I'll tell you all about it. I'm Aureus," he adds,
holding out his other hand to shake. His fingers are decorated

with tattoos of runic symbols and he wears several rings with precious gems.

I take his hand and say, "Jace."

He walks us toward the inn and steers us down a side alley. The alley seems unassuming enough, but as soon as Aureus knocks a rhythm on a brick wall, a door appears and slides open. Yet again, I am forced to come to terms with the fact that things are never as they seem. I shake my head and walk through the doorway. I do not know what I expected, but we are greeted by a relatively normal-looking pub. A woman behind the bar shouts a greeting to him as we enter and he waves a hand lazily. Drinks are pressed into our hands as we make our way to a table in the back corner, where it is quietest. I sip at my drink and a delicious, citrusy taste bursts across my palate.

"Let's see it, then," Aureus says, teasingly impatient. I shoot him a puzzled look and he says, "Your mark! Every person who has been chosen has a mark left on them by their God or Goddess." He holds out his wrist and shows me a wreath of laurel leaves tattooed like a bracelet. "I was chosen by the Emperor God," he tells me.

I hold out my hand and show him the purple flower on my thumb. "I'm not sure what it is or what it means," I admit, taking another deep drink.

"Moonflower," he tells me. "You've been chosen by Karishua, the Goddess of Fate. You must be on some life path," he says with a whistle. I absently trace the flower on my thumb as I listen to him speak. "In the history that has been documented, Karishua has only chosen four other humans. She does not choose lightly. "

"So what does that mean for me?" I ask him, suddenly nervous. Somehow, I've gone from believing in no deity to being guarded and chosen by some mysterious, apparently incredible being. "How do I honor her? What do I need to do? I don't...I've never believed in this stuff before."

"She'll tell you, when it is time," Aureus says. "Until then, continue the way you have been, but allow for the tides of change to mold you. And, when in doubt, bottoms up," he adds, downing his mead and smacking his lips loudly. I grin and follow suit.

I follow him as he shows me around the village. Before I know it, the sun has slipped away and the village is aglow with lanterns and fires. Aureus is pulled aside by a few of his friends, and I wander alone until the fires and the sounds fade into the background. A dark expanse stretches between the village and where I will be headed come morning, another copse of trees and the general unknown. I gave up hope of knowing what I would be walking into quite some time ago. For tonight, though, I decide to let myself enjoy a real bed, a real meal, and the first decent company I have had in ages.

As I lay in bed, my muscles all seizing and stretching in an attempt to adjust to the sudden comfort, I stroke the moonflower on my thumb. It is illuminated by the light of the full moon that streams through the window. I do not know what it means for me to have been chosen, or why I would be the one Karishua chose, but it brings me a small comfort to know that perhaps I have someone or something out there watching over me.

In the morning, I stop back at the temple before I leave Caroleam. I settle myself once more on the cushion and close my eyes. In all honesty, I feel like a fool. Never once have I meditated, nor have I placed stock in gods and goddesses. I crack one eye open and look around the temple, but nothing has changed. With a huff, I open both of my eyes and stare at the bowl of moonflowers in front of me. Is it rude if I leave? Eventually, I need to get moving. I uncross my legs and stand with my hands on my hips.

"Well, you can't say I didn't try," I tell the bowl of flowers. I turn on my heel and leave, the heavy doors thudding shut behind me. Aureus is there again and I am surprised to see him.

"Call me the guardian of the temple," he offers. "Are you leaving so soon?"

"I have to," I say. "I need to find my sister. I need to figure out what the hell is going on around me."

"If you figure that out, you tell me how," he says. "I'm still working on figuring that out for myself."

"You've got yourself a deal," I tell him, holding out a hand.

He takes mine and shakes it firmly. "Thank you, for everything," I add with sincere gratitude. "I hope to cross paths with you again someday."

"You're welcome in Alymere any time. My home court," he clarifies at my look

"Alymere," I repeat thoughtfully, "I will be sure to remember that." We both nod and then I am off once more, disappearing into the trees. For some time, I am able to see the golden statue at the top of the temple. Eventually, though, it disappears behind the treetops. I trudge forward, praying for a quick and problem-free crossing into Apaiji.

I can tell the moment I near the border between Kydier and Apaiji. The air becomes heavy with humidity, and the heat continues to climb. The lush deciduous trees through which I was stalking before have become sparse and now disappear completely. I make my way carefully down a rocky mountainside that is covered in green, fern-like plants and wildflowers. The mountains turn to cliffs, and are treacherous in how smooth they are; their smoothness means no foot- or handholds. Slow and steady wins it, and I clamber down the rocks like a newborn calf. There is a thin river snaking between the cavernous cliffs, and I can see an occasional boat here and there with one or two passengers aboard. I wonder if this is an option for me, as well.

In spite of the dangers of the cliffside and the potential enemies I may meet at the end of my climb, Kydier has proven to be a beautiful land. In fact, I have not once seen anything near to what we have been taught to believe in Battlewood. The way our historians spin it, the outside courts are barren wastelands, filled with poverty and violence. We have been taught that the surrounding courts defy our very way of existence, and this is true—they do. But I'm learning over and over again that different does not mean dangerous; different means interesting, exciting and daring. And frankly, I think Battlewood could do with some changing. Maybe Aleca knew more than I gave her credit for.

Finally, I reach the bottom of the cliff and jump down onto the solid ground. My hands sting with minute cuts on my palms, and my leg muscles are burning from exertion. I shield my eyes with a hand as I survey the area around me. Technically, I could swim across the lake and continue to walk that side, but I do not know where it would lead. I cannot see beyond the curve of the cliffs. I seat myself and pull out some of the meager rations I have left, along with some of the calendula poultice Willow gave me before we left. I was able to find a few soup balls, mercifully, but they do not do me any good when I am unable to cook. With luck, I'll find more welcoming hosts in Apaiji than I have found at the vagabond village in Kydier. I rub some of the poultice into my palms, and almost instantly, the stinging is gone. I am almost certain I can watch the cuts seal themselves. I shake my head, cap the jar of poultice, and set it aside in favor of a meal.

Nibbling on the last of my jerky and dried fruits, I re-examine the map created by Willow and the map that Aleca has sealed into her notebook. It is difficult to believe that I have travelled so far from my home. Although I was trained as a warrior, my duties were surrounding the perimeter of my land or minding the prisoners. While it is true that Battlewood and the courts around us signed the Pact of Silence, it has not stopped foreigners from attempting to come into our court. Battlewood has more enemies than it does friends.

I stretch out my stiff muscles and rise with a groan. If I am to find Aleca, I would be better served moving along the land instead of sitting like a duck. The only problem is, I have no idea where to go from here. I am alone but for the birds in the sky and the sounds of the water lapping the sides of the shore.

"Jace Grimme of Battlewood. We have been waiting for you."

I whip around, drawing my dagger as I turn, and come face-to-face with a woman who stands with her hands up and open—presumably to show me she means no harm. I do not lower my blade as we look each other over. I consider throwing the blade and running, but then I would be without a weapon. Worse yet, I might end up arming her with my blade and leave myself defenseless. I weigh the options quickly before deciding to speak.

"Who are you?" I demand.

She keeps her hands up as she replies, "My name is Bronwyn.

I am Seer to Empress Luna, of Apaiji. I have been sent to bring you safely into our courts." Her voice is low, almost musical; it has a similar quality to the voices of the sirens from before and it makes me uneasy.

"How do I know you're telling the truth?" I ask her. "Why should I believe you?"

"You do not have to believe me, Jace," Bronwyn says, "but I assure you I speak true. Your search for your sister draws to an end; I can help you finish this quest. Your sister is right—you are as different as night and day, though no less passionate." Her eyes are earnest as she stares at me. I have to look away— they are too similar to Willow's for comfort.

"You've seen Aleca?" I ask. "When? Is she okay? Where is she?"

"Come with me and see for yourself," Bronwyn offers.

I mentally race through the pros and cons. The way I see it, I'm taking a risk either way. I can go alone and try to figure it out on my own, or I can go with this stranger who claims to be sent to help me. The fact that she knows who I am, and what I've been sent to do, does nothing to quell my discomfort. It is not her knowledge to have, and I feel set on edge. I chew on my lip as I try to make a decision.

"Where are we?" I ask, picturing my map in my head.

"The Letonas Tides," Bronwyn says, "the sea connecting all islands to Apaiji. Across this sea is the way to the heart of our world."

I shift my grip on the blade, still wary of the woman in front of me. This sea may tie the courts together, but it would also be a convenient place to drown someone and make it look like an accident. Having been on the other side of covering up deaths once too many times before, I am hesitant to accept anything she says. Plenty of people have been tricked into their own deaths in the past. The fact that she seems kind and helpful means nothing to me.

"Why do you want to help me?" I finally question. "You don't know me."

"The Empress does," Bronwyn says. "Karishua, your Goddess, does. And I have Seen you coming for some time now. We have been waiting for your arrival."

"Who is 'we'?"

"Me. The Empress. Your sister. I can help make this quest easier," Bronwyn offers to me. "I am not here to make false promises. You may take my help or leave it." In what I assume is a show of good faith, she settles herself into a kneeling position; I could kill her easily if I so chose. We both know that it would be a cold-blooded kill, though.

"Alright," I agree slowly, sheathing my dagger again. "But if you try to pull anything on me, I won't go down without a fight."

"I would expect nothing less from a warrior," she says. "I know you do not trust me yet, but you will."

"I doubt it," I mutter. She rises and begins to walk, not

waiting to see if I follow after her. I should have taken a blood oath from her first. I have no way to prove that she is who she says she is. I still have no way to prove that she won't try to harm me. Linota would be less than impressed with some of the decisions I have made lately. I have been bringing shame to the name of the warrior. Is it too late to make an oath? I consider pricking my finger and grabbing hold of her, but do not.

In spite of my irritation, I take note of who this woman is. She is dressed similarly to how I would dress at home: linen pants, a tunic, and a leather harness around her shoulders. However, instead of weapons in the harness, it is stocked with bottles, rolls of fabric, and tins. Our feet send pebbles scattering as we walk and I kick some away. "What do you mean, you're a Seer?"

"I See," Bronwyn answers me. My disparaging look is wasted on the back of her head.

"Yes, I figured out that part," I say in annoyance. "What does that mean?"

"I have the ability to See the future and the present. What is happening in the world around us. I cannot see pasts," she says. "Not unless what happened in your past directly influenced your future." I scoff and she looks over her shoulder at me. "You do not place much faith in these things, I know. You will in time."

She leads me around the bend of the cliff, and we come to

the mouth of an ocean. From the shoreline, I can see islands peppering the water. A large ship is anchored in the surf. The sails are turquoise and emblazoned with a symbol completely foreign to me. There is no end of the water in sight, and I stifle a groan.

We make our way onto the ship, where we are greeted by two women dressed in boldly-patterned skirts and strapless tops decorated with rows of jingling metal coins. They bow to us as we pass them, and Bronwyn bows back. I nod my head at them, unsure what custom dictates. I feel like a specimen under a glass as I pass by the people milling about the ship. I am highly aware of how grimy and dirty I appear in contrast to their crisp, clean appearances. I attempt to wipe some of the dirt off of my hands and face and come away with darker streaks than before. Bronwyn seems to pay no mind to this as we cross the deck and enter into a captain's suite. She sweeps into the room and hops up onto a large table.

"I have found her," she says as she crosses her ankles. "And she has provided much less of a fight than expected."

"She's standing right here, you know," I grumble, "and she hasn't ruled it out yet." I look around the suite curiously. One wall is lined with books and artifacts on shelves. Opposite that wall, a massive map is spread out, showing intricacies of the Nautilus of Courts, as well as the surrounding lands outside of the Nautilus. It would appear that this world is much larger than what Battlewood would have ever taught its citizens to believe. Battlewood has lied to us yet again. What a surprise.

"Yes, of course," Bronwyn says. She slides down off of the table and beckons me toward her. "Captain Talolyn, Jace Grimme. Jace, Captain Talolyn."

"It's about time we found ye," a gravelly voice says. "We've been searchin' for almost a fortnight, since yer sis came." A man steps out of the shadows and into the center of the room. His voice does not match his appearance in the slightest. I am nearly eye-level with the man; he is small and scrawny, with a scar on his left cheek and barely a wisp of hair on his head. A scraggly beard covers most of his mouth, but his eyes are bright and friendly. He looks as if a single puff of wind could knock him over and break him into a hundred pieces. In spite of this, his handshake is firm and energetic.

"I don't understand. Why have you been looking for me?" I ask.

"There'll be plenty o' time for questions later, miss," Talolyn says. "If I ain't mistaken, you'll be wantin' some clean clothes and a bit to eat, hmm? Bronwyn'll see to it. Go on, now. I've a ship to sail." He waves us away, and Bronwyn leads me out of his cabin.

"Talolyn is…eccentric," she tells me. "He is worth his weight in gold as a captain, but useless if you want information. Although he was right about one thing," she adds thoughtfully.

"What's that?" I ask.

"We should get you a bath and some clean clothes. Come with me."

...... † ......

Bronwyn leads me to a cabin that I assume has been laid out in readiness for me. A large tub, hidden by a clever folding screen, is filled with steaming water. Dark flecks of something—I cannot tell what—float on the top. Beside it rests a table covered by tubs of scented goo. I pick up each jar and sniff them delicately. Each one smells different.

"Your clothes have been laid out for you on your bed. You should find that they are your size. Dispose of the clothing you are wearing now. I will be with Captain Talolyn, when you are ready," Bronwyn tells me.

As she leaves, I begin to undress. My clothing has seen better days. The soles of my boots are shredded and all of the tread has worn away. My tunic is stained with dirt, sweat, and blood; my pants are not much better. I drop it all into a pile and turn to face the tub of water. Tentatively, I scoop up some of the water and examine it closely. Upon closer inspection, the flecks are herbs. I should have figured. I drop the water back into the tub and then submerge my entire body in the water, closing my eyes as I sink underneath. I take my time letting the water wash over me, and by the time I have finished, my skin is wrinkled like a prune.

Once I have bathed and dried, I examine the clothing that has been set out for me. I am expecting another pair of breeches and a tunic, and instead, find that a dress and strappy sandals have been provided. It is nothing like the clothing that

I wore in Garyn. This dress comes to rest at my knees and is made of two panels of brown suede and a middle panel of patterned fabric. It is a sleeveless garment, and I am relieved to find that the shoulder straps are wide and comfortable, not string like in Garyn.

The one downfall to this outfit is that there is nowhere for me to keep my weapon on hand. It falls out of the straps in the sandals, and there are no pockets in this dress. Reluctantly, I tuck the blade safely into my bag and stow the whole lot beneath my cot. I stare longingly at the cot and then find my way back to the captain's suite. Bronwyn and Talolyn are deep in conversation but they cease talking immediately as I enter. It is evident that I was the topic of conversation. I do not speak immediately, instead, busying myself with the books stuffed into shelves. When I finally turn around, both Talolyn and Bronwyn are watching me.

"May I help you?" I ask them. I do not appreciate being watched, and it has my defenses up.

"Are you hungry?" Bronwyn asks. She motions to a table set for three, laden down with an assortment of food. "We usually gather to eat together with the rest of the crew and passengers, but we've made an allowance in your case."

"We figured ye'd wanny eat away from peerin' eyes teday," Talolyn says, sitting at the table and tucking a cloth into the collar of his tunic. He tears into a leg of chicken without another word and jerks his head to an empty chair beside him.

Slowly, I pull the chair out and take a seat. Bronwyn seats herself across from me and gives me a small smile before filling her plate with food.

"You have not made this journey alone," Bronwyn says. "Where is your fire-haired companion?"

"Shouldn't your mind-reading be able to tell you?" I ask, my mood souring again quickly. Of all the things I would like to talk about, my lonely status is not one of them. It seems to be a talent of mine to lose the people who are closest to me.

"I do not read minds, Jace," Bronwyn says calmly. "I See what is to come, and what is here. She is instrumental in your life. Your work together is not done."

"Yeah, well, she's not here anymore, so it doesn't matter, does it?" I stab at a carrot on my plate as I speak. Eager to change the subject, I ask, "You said you've been looking for me. Why?"

"We canny answer that yet, lass," Talolyn says. "Ye'll have to wait until we dock at Apaiji."

"Why?" I ask again.

"You must wait," Bronwyn says. She does not expound this. I take a deep breath and let it out slowly, measuring my annoyance before I allow myself to speak.

"Is there anything that you can tell me?" I ask, fighting to keep my voice even.

"Jace, you must–,"

"–Wait? Yeah, I've got it," I snap. Pinching the bridge of my nose, I take another deep breath to steady my temper.

"Am sorry, lass," Talolyn says apologetically with a clap on my shoulder. "I know it's gotta be frustratin'. We'll be on land before ye know it, though. Ye look awfully familiar, ye know. Ye and yer sis both. Yer sure I never sailed ye?"

"I'm positive. You must be mistaking us with someone else. If you'll excuse me. I think I'll turn in for the night," I say, pushing myself away from the table and rising.

As I pull the door open and exit, I hear Bronwyn say, "She carries so much inside her. If only she'd share her burden."

I laugh humorlessly as the door snaps shut behind me. With whom would I share anything? There are only three people in my life who matter, and all three are gone.

...... † ......

The bitter tears begin to fall before I can make it to my room. I collapse onto a bench on the deck of the ship. Alone and surrounded by strangers in foreign waters, the exhaustion washes over me in waves. I am tired and alone. My mind cannot turn off. My body aches with over-exertion and poor nutritional intake. My heart aches for my parents, for my sister, for Tally, for Willow. I wish my parents were alive; it has been eight years since I lost them. I wonder what they would say to me. I wish my sister was with me. I wish I hadn't walked away from Willow. I wish, I wish, I wish...

I double over and bury my head in my hands. How can so much have changed in such a short period of time? I had a secure future with the warriors of Battlewood; I knew what my motivations were, and I did not question them. Now, I question everything that ever meant anything to me. I cannot even say I know who I am anymore. If it weren't for my absolute focus on finding Aleca, what would be the purpose to my existence? Nothing is tying me down to anything. What if I just continue to float for the rest of my days? I always thought that I was protecting myself by not allowing anyone to get close to me. It turns out I was just hurting myself instead.

I think back to what Klara told me in her kitchen. I am like stone, and I must be more like water. I did not fully understand what she meant then; I am beginning to see now, though. None of these changes within me have come easily. I always teased and scolded Aleca for thinking with her heart instead of her head, but it appears that she had it right from the start. It is not an easy transition to become less like stone. There is a part of me that wants to quit now, to retreat back within my old ways. There is another part, however, that knows I can never go back. I can only go forward.

I cannot say what I will find. I cannot say who I will become. All I can say is who I have been—and that person who I no longer wish to be.

after the last fall

SEVEN

I do not remember making my way back into my cabin, but I must have done so. When I wake, sun is pouring through the porthole and into the room. It takes me a moment to gather my bearings. I am not accustomed to spending extended periods of time on the water, and my stomach roils queasily. I rifle through my bags for something—anything—that will settle my stomach. My hands come away empty, and I settle with deep breaths through my nose. I should have taken Willow up on her offer to make more remedies. There are a lot of things that I should have done differently, now that I think about it.

With a sigh, I rise from my bed and search for clothing to wear. While I did not dislike the dress from yesterday, I prefer to wear pants. I am down to my last pair of breeches, and I make a note to find some more in Apaiji. It would not do to make my way back to Battlewood in a skirt. As soon as I have dressed, I leave in search of Talolyn. I do not know my way around this ship, and if anyone can help me, it is him.

I am able to make my way back to his quarters. I knock on the door and am greeted by Talolyn's weathered, smiling face.

"Mornin' lass," he greets me. "What can I do for ye?"

"I…," I trail off, gnawing my lip. "I'm not sure," I say at last.

He steps back and jerks his head, inviting me in. I follow him into his quarters but stop at the sight of Bronwyn seated at a table. Spending my morning with her was not on my list of things that I wanted to do today. Cards are laid out in front of her, and she stares at them intensely. She does not look up as Talolyn and I move past her. As we do, I notice that the cards have images on them. They are nothing like the playing cards I have used around the fire with my fellow warriors. Talolyn presses a finger to his lips and motions to her.

Twice, she lets out a sigh and shuffles the cards before laying them out in the same pattern. I do not know what she is doing, but it appears to make sense to her. Bronwyn murmurs something unintelligible before scooping the cards up and placing them back in her deck. She looks up at me and nods.

"You wonder what that was," she says. I make a non-committal shrug. "Tarot," she tells me. "Reading what has happened and what is to come through the cards."

I cannot stifle the scoff that I let out. "How can cards tell you any of that?" I ask her. She motions for me to sit across from her, and I do. She lifts the deck of cards again and offers them to me. I take them and examine them doubtfully. None of the pictures make any sense to me. I have a hard time believing that pictures could tell the past or the future. "There is no way to know the future until it happens." I sift through the cards as I speak and one falls out of the deck. Before I can pick it up, Bronwyn snatches it and stares at it for a moment.

"Queen of Swords," she says, holding it up for me to see.

I look at it, not understanding what I am supposed to be seeing. "Is that supposed to mean something?" I finally ask. I take the card from her hand and scrutinize it: a woman holds a sword in front of her face, covering her right eye. Though it is only a drawing, the left eye stares at me with a piercing gaze.

"What do you feel from it?" Bronwyn asks, turning my question back on me.

My instinct is to say, "Nothing," but I know that is not the case. I am drawn to the card in spite of my misgivings. "She seems…determined. Maybe a little calculating," I say. "Cold? I don't know." I push the card back across the table to Bronwyn.

"She is you," Bronwyn tells me. "It fell for a reason." She looks at the card, and then at me. "You rule with intellect and reason, instead of with emotion. You tell it like it is; whether this is a good or bad thing, I do not know. The Queen of Swords is ruled by air, which pushes away the outside obstacles to get to the meaning of things." She pauses and then says, "Be careful not to shut off your emotions completely. You need to discern with ease, but you must not allow yourself to ignore your heart completely. You have been through difficult times. It is time for change." She shuffles the cards again, rifling through them. "Would you like a reading?"

"No, thank you. That was quite enough," I say, rising. "I'm going to go for a walk." I leave before either of them can say another word.

I feel rankled by Bronwyn's words. She has confirmed what I already knew was my weakness, and it leaves me feeling irritated and ashamed. It is a theme that has appeared over and over in the past months: be less like stone, show more emotion, do not be so cold. It is a difficult thing to come to terms with; I spent the first sixteen years of my life being told that to be emotional and vulnerable is to be weak. However, I can no longer deny that changes have taken root inside of me and are beginning to grow. Perhaps it is not so clear to those around me. I feel much less detached from people, and I remember now why I began to detach in the first place. Placing myself in their hands only sets me up for hurt and failure later. If I do not attach, I cannot care when it ultimately falls apart.

My feet carry me aimlessly around the deck of the ship. I can see the beginnings of land in the distance; I can only hope that this is the border of Apaiji. I do not care what I find when I get there. Part of me hopes that I am wrong and that Aleca is not actually there. It would certainly save me the trouble of having to bring her all the way back to Battlewood. I would not have to return. It is a shock to my system to discover that I feel intrigued and not unhappy about this. The land I once revered now repulses me. Of course, with this revelation, it is driven even further home that I am now a drifter, with nowhere and no one to call my home. Perhaps I can request a mercy kill once we land in Apaiji, a penance for Battlewood's wrongdoings. Or perhaps for my own wrongdoings. I have no shortage of those.

Sometimes I wonder what would have happened with Aleca if I had not behaved the way I did after our parents died. Would she have still tried so hard to enter into other lands? Would she have held so tightly to the idea of magic, exploration, and change? Did she cling to the ideas because she was left to her own devices so much? I know I did not make her childhood any easier, and I was the one who was supposed to take on caring for her. I feel that Battlewood should shoulder some of the blame—who expects a fifteen-year-old to raise their little sister? I wonder what would happen in Garyn in that situation. I assume the village would come together to help raise an orphan. But this is not the way in Battlewood. In Battlewood, it is every man for himself, and if you break the law, then to hell with you.

I lean over the railing, hands clasped together, and watch the water lap at the sides of the ship. For just a moment, I think about what would happen if I were to jump over the rail and into the water. Would Aleca be safe, or would Raznik send someone else after her instead? Would Willow ever know what happened? Would it be quick and painless, or slow and torturous? It wouldn't matter. No matter the course to get there, eventually it would all end, anyway. And wouldn't that be my goal? To take away the constant roar of thoughts, the constant tightness in my chest?

Of course, I do not go through with it. I am a coward, despite what I may present to others. I know that I live a lie every single day. For years, I was able to build a fortress around myself in order to present a strong face, emotionless and detached. I have fought so hard to quell my emotions. It is so much easier to turn yourself off to the world around you than to be barraged with fears and dreams and everything in between. It was easier, until Willow came around.

Willow, my proverbial chisel; she has no idea what effect she had on me. From the moment I began my training as a warrior, I swore I would never again take down my defenses. As I saw it, I wouldn't have to live that way for a long time—warriors are not known for their long lifespan. If I am honest, I chose that role deliberately. I hoped it would bring a quicker end, and save me from having to face the end of my life in a different way. But all of that began to unravel when Willow worked her way into my world. And then, in a breath, she was gone, and all I had was broken walls and no way to fix them again. I don't know who I hate more: myself, for allowing that to happen; or Raznik, for sending me out here in the first place. I've tried to hate Willow, but I cannot. There is a constant dull ache in my chest. I miss her.

I am so wrapped in my own thoughts that I do not hear Bronwyn approach me. I startle as she comes to stand next to me. She hands me a cloth with some bread and fruit wrapped inside.

"You hurried away before you could eat," she tells me. "You must keep up your strength." I take the cloth from her, eyeing the multi-colored fruit with apprehension. It is red and green and covered in spikes. It is like nothing I have ever seen before. "It is a fruit known to our lands," Bronwyn explains. "Dragonfruit, we call it. It grows nowhere but Apaiji."

"Are we near Apaiji at all?" I ask, nibbling at the white meat of the fruit. When I decide I like the taste, I take a larger bite.

"We should make landfall by tomorrow afternoon," Bronwyn says. "We will have to make a stop along the way to see the Empress," she adds. "We must see about getting you a new wardrobe."

"No dresses," I request. "I'd feel more comfortable in breeches or…or something."

Bronwyn regards me for a moment, thinking, and then nods. "Yes, that will do," she says, "though you will need to wear a ceremonial gown in order to meet with the Empress."

"Who exactly is this Empress?" I ask, tearing a chunk of bread off and eating it.

"She rules Apaiji," Bronwyn says. "We are a matriarchal society. We have always been ruled by an Empress. It was deigned to be so at the Mountains of the Goddess many centuries ago. It has never failed us, and will never fail us." She leans against the railing, her back to the water. "It wouldn't have solved anything, you know."

"What?" I ask, confused by the sudden change in topic.

"If you had jumped into the water," Bronwyn says softly, "it wouldn't have solved anything. It would have made things even worse, for your sister and for Willow. For Battlewood as a whole. You do not know it yet, but you are key to what happens in Battlewood in the coming months."

"I wasn't going to jump," I say stiffly. It is not the first time I have gotten the impression that Bronwyn can do more than just read the future, and it unsettles me. My mind is my own, and I do not like that she can poke around in it.

"Well, I am glad about that," she says. "I like you. I know we do not see eye-to-eye on most things–,"

"–anything–,"

"–but even so, I do like you. You are more important than you realize." She does not say anything else, and we stand side-by-side in silence.

I battle internally for a moment before asking, "Can you…See Willow?" I hate how weak and hopeful it makes me sound, but I cannot help myself. I know that Aleca is safe, and that Bronwyn has made contact with her. But Willow…I left Willow behind to find her way home on her own.

"Indeed I can," Bronwyn says. "Would you like me to show you?" She motions to a smooth piece of black glass tied at her waist. I shake my head quickly.

"N-no," I say, "I just want to be sure…" I trail off, unsure of how to finish.

"Willow is safe," Bronwyn says. "You trained her well."

"I didn't–,"

"She was watching you closely, whether you realize it or not. You taught her many new things," she tells me. "It seems she did the same for you."

"Is there any chance that you'll stop reading my mind at any point in the near future?" I ask in annoyance—although I find there is not as much heart behind it as usual.

"It is not likely," she says unapologetically. There is a hint of glee to her voice.

"I didn't think so," I say, taking another bite of the exotic fruit and focusing once more on the approaching shoreline.

······ † ······

When we finally make landfall, I want to cry with relief. Despite my feet being firmly planted on the dock, I feel myself pitching back and forth as if still on the water. There is a bustling of people as we all make our way off of the ship and toward the dusty path that leads to a city. It is evident that this is a seaport town; there are many ships and smaller boats docked at the shoreline, barrels of fish, and the persistent cries of birds in the air. People are calling to one another as they draw in their nets and load wagons filled with goods and wares. I make myself dizzy as I whirl around to take it all in. I stop only at the sight of four people convened on a large rock jutting into the water.

They hold hands in a circle, chanting something I cannot make out. Multi-colored sparks fly from the center of their circle before fizzling out completely. The smoke begins to form a hazy image, and before long, I am staring at the smoke-outline of a large tree. I rub my eyes, certain they are playing a trick on me, but when my vision clears, the tree still hangs in the air. I can feel my mouth drop open in surprise, and I point at the smoke, now dissipating.

"What…how–they–there was a–what?" I splutter incredulously.

"There was a what?" Bronwyn asks calmly.

"A tree! There were sparks and singing and then the smoke made a picture? A tree, in the smoke! How?" I cannot control the frenzy in my voice.

"A tree? Interesting," she says in a thoughtful voice. "Do you know what kind?"

I am about to say no when I remember the long, wispy branches of the tree, swaying to and fro. With a knot in my stomach, I nod. "A willow," I say with difficulty. "Didn't you see it?"

"I did not see a tree at all," Bronwyn says. "I saw something else entirely."

"How is that possible?" I ask.

"The sea is a conduit for magic," Bronwyn says. "Those who

are searching for something gather here each day, waiting for the smoke weavers to assist in their journey. I did not realize I was searching for something," she adds quietly. "Most interesting."

I shake my head, grabbing my pack and hitching it on my shoulder. There is already so much to learn about this land, and I have not even left the dock. I rack my brain, trying to remember what we were taught about Apaiji. All that comes to mind is that Apaiji is filled with dangerous people and is a wild and chaotic place. From what I can see, though, this does not fit that description at all. People chat happily with one another as they gather their goods and pack their wagons. Some are whistling jaunty tunes as they walk. There is a definite din— bells from the ships, a myriad of voices, crashing of waves— but none of it strikes me as dangerous in the least. More and more, I question what Battlewood is trying to hide from its people.

We make our way up the dusty path. It begins to climb slightly, and then opens up into the city itself. In the distance, beyond the city, I can see a citadel gleaming in the bright sun. I have never been to a place like this before, and I wish I had a hundred more eyes to see everything at once. The city is awash in gold, turquoise, and purple mosaics. There are pubs, inns, and stores lining the paths. Kiosks boasting crystals, books, wands, and dried herbs are set up along the way. Twice, a stranger passes a stone into my hand and hurries away without a word. Goldstone and blue lace agate, Bronwyn calls them. I do not understand what their purposes are, but they are beautiful nonetheless, and I tuck them safely inside my breast pocket.

Bronwyn seems to know most everyone she passes. They all greet her cheerfully, and she waves back with a serene smile. At the very center of the city, a massive golden fountain spouts water. The metal has been shaped into a crescent moon with a large jewel hanging off of the tip. The jewel reflects the sun into the water and throws prisms of color across the surrounding area. I can see coins shimmering underneath the water and point them out to Bronwyn.

"Yes, it is our wishing fountain," Bronwyn tells me. "The intent is attached to the coin and then thrown into the water for the gods and goddesses to hear. Many wishes have been granted this way. If your wish is denied, your coin will show up in your home. Would you like to try?" she asks me, handing me an odd silver coin.

I run a finger over the symbol worked into the face of it. "What harm could it do?" I ask. I think for a moment about what my wish is, and then cast it into the water. I suppose only time will tell if my wish has been heard.

...... † ......

We come to a stop just outside of an elaborate gate. The crescent moon and jewel symbol have been planted here, as well. It is through these gates that we will enter the citadel. My body feels alive with nerves—there is so little distance now between me and my sister. I have not seen her in so long, and I am anxious to reunite with her. Has she changed? Is she still my Aleca, or someone different? Will she even want to see me? I take deep breaths to steady myself. Bronwyn has left to go speak with a guard at the gate, and I am impatient as I stand before the doors. And then, with a single bell toll, the gates begin to open, and Bronwyn rejoins me.

"We have only one last stop before you may see your sister," she tells me. We step through the gates, and I inhale sharply. There is another small city within these gates. Small groups of twos and threes are clustered together, heads bent over parchment, books, and small fire stands. Every once in a while, an older person wanders over and makes suggestions or corrections. I watch curiously, and Bronwyn says, "The academy is within these walls. They are all studying some form of magic."

"Why is the academy hidden behind…this?" I ask, motioning to the now-closed gates and tall stucco walls.

"Not everyone is picked for the life of magic," she says. "Some are chosen, and some are not. I studied here. I was chosen some time ago, and was sent to Apaiji for training."

"You're not from here?" I ask, surprised. She shakes her head.

"I am from Kydier, originally," she tells me. "Now, I serve the Empress. Come, we must get you ready. We have already taken too long."

Bronwyn leads me to a small cottage tucked just beyond the gates. The garden is filled with overflowing flowerbeds and hanging chimes. It is a comfortable home, and briefly, I picture myself living somewhere like this. Would I be happy here? Would I always feel like something was missing? More and more, I feel that I know myself less. Perhaps I should just start anew as a different person. I think that I could make it work for me. I think I would like to be separated from the Jace I used to be.

Bronwyn pushes the door open and invites me to go in first. "Is this your home?" I ask as I enter the main room. There are books surrounded by torn and crumpled papers, half-melted candles, and various pieces of jet black glass. It is clearly her workplace. I move to touch the glass, and then pull back. I don't know anything about these things, and I am not foolish enough to rush in head-first. If I have learned anything over the past few months, it is that magic most certainly exists, and I know approximately nothing about it. I will have to be sure to tell Aleca that I am now a believer.

"Yes," Bronwyn says. "We need to cleanse and purify ourselves before we enter the Empress's space. Follow me to the bathing area, and I will show you what to do." She leads me toward the back of the cottage. There is already a tub filled with steaming water, and I wonder if someone knew we were coming. Beside it, much like on the ship, there is a table laden with creams, soaps, and something that looks like crystals of sugar mixed with herbs and oil. "Wash with the soaps, and then use this cream when you use the blade. After–"

"I'm sorry, when I use the what?" I ask. As far as I'm concerned, blades are for maiming. Never have I taken a blade to my bathing ritual.

"The blade. It is a tool of purification before seeing the Empress Luna," Bronwyn says. "It is used as a means to clear oneself of the imperfections that have captured impurities in the past, and to allow for newness in its place."

"What am I supposed to do with it?" I ask, picking it up and staring at it. "I'm not drawing blood for someone I don't even know." I cannot think of any other way a blade could be used for purification. Blood purification is a common ritual in Battlewood—one I have been subjected to both willingly and unwillingly. Now is not one of those willing times, and I am ready to continue the fight. Bronwyn takes it from me and holds it flat to her arm. In one motion, she pulls it upward, bringing away the light fuzz on her arms.

"Arms, legs, and under your arms," she directs me.

"That makes no sense," I argue. "That hair grows for a reason. In the winter–"

"It is not winter here, and it is the custom of our lands. It is necessary if you wish to meet with Empress Luna and see your sister again. The choice is yours," Bronwyn says. She holds out the blade for me in the palm of her hand. I take it back with a sigh. Despite what she says, I know that I truly do not have a choice in this. "When you have finished with the blade, use this scrub to complete the process. I will set out your gown." She leaves without another word, and I am left staring warily at the blade. I sigh again and begin the purification process. I have to maneuver carefully around the not-quite-healed scars on my arms in order to avoid cutting them open. I do well with this until I move on to my legs. I nick my knees and my left ankle, and hiss as blood runs down my leg like a grisly watercolor. If I never have to do this again, I will not be upset.

Finally, I am finished. I feel no more pure and cleansed than I did when I entered Bronwyn's home; I do not understand how this was supposed to have made a difference. I stare at my reflection in the mirror on the wall, trying to see if there is any change. My gaze falls on the blade in the mirrored glass, and I reach for it. I narrow my eyes, staring at my hair for a moment, and then bring the blade up. It takes some effort, but I am able to shape the edges and give myself feathery bangs that go across my forehead. The end result is quite satisfying, and it now looks like a deliberate style instead of a desperate trade.

My clothing has been set in front of the bathing space, and I unfold it gently. Despite my general dislike of gowns, I cannot help but be impressed by this. The gown is floor-length and made with gentle swaths of silver-lilac chiffon. A bodice of chainmail turns into a high collar and armored shoulder caps. I run my fingers along the fabric in awe. It is even more beautiful on, and I cannot stop staring at myself in it. I feel transformed. A soft knock makes me whirl around. Bronwyn stands in the entryway holding a long string of spikes.

"For your hair," she tells me. "You have changed your cut. It suits you." She enters the room and crosses to me. "May I?" she asks. I nod, and she sets to work on my short strands. It reminds me so much of when Willow worked my hair that I have to press my fist to my stomach to dull the ache. After a moment, Bronwyn has finished, and I look at her handiwork. The spikes are woven in and out of a braid that wraps around my head as a crown. Other than this simple braid, my hair is untouched. She rings my eyes in black kohl and then steps back.

"Are we ready?" I ask.

"We are," she confirms. "Let us not keep Empress Luna waiting any longer."

...... † ......

We are greeted at the top of the citadel steps by a man. He is quite possibly the most intimidating man I have ever met, with rippling muscles and a stoic face. His skin, a warm brown, shows no signs of imperfections. Except for the neatly trimmed beard on his face, he has no hair. He wears no jewelry, except for a thick gold hoop in one ear. Teal cloth is wrapped around his wrists to his forearms. Besides this, he is shirtless. In fact, the only clothing he wears is a pair of cloth breeches and soft leather boots. There is only one long blade tucked into a sheath on his left hip. I get the impression that he would be quick and deadly with that one, lone weapon.

Despite whatever intimidation I feel, Bronwyn strides right up to him and gives a little bow.

"Bronwyn," the man says. His voice is like thunder, and I can feel it reverberate against my chest.

"Obsidian," she greets him. "This is Jace Grimme." She motions to me, and he eyes me over her shoulder. I smile nervously, and he steps toward me.

"Jace," he says. And then his face splits into a wide smile. "It's nice to put a face to the name. We have heard quite a bit about you. My name is Obsidian Black. I am the right-hand man to Empress Luna. I've been asked to bring you to her." He holds out a hand, and I shake it. The strength in his grip nearly brings me to my knees. With a laugh, he bids Bronwyn and me to follow him through the doors.

My nervousness grows with each step I take. I have no idea what I am walking into; the only thing of which I am certain is that it is going to be entirely foreign to me. While I am growing more accustomed to the idea of magic, I cannot pretend that I am comfortable with it—and here, I am surrounded by it on all sides. The air nearly hums with the magic it contains. It is as opposite to Battlewood as night is to day.

In fact, Apaiji is the antithesis of Battlewood. Where our castle is grey, bleak, and cold, Apaiji's is gold, glittering with jewels, and bursting with color. People do not keep their heads bowed as they scurry through the hall, but rather they greet each other and stop to talk. There is no sense of foreboding. It is remarkable to me that it has taken me so long to see Battlewood for what it truly is. I wonder how I will ever be able to return there. And when I do, what will I find?

The long hallway leading to the Empress is decorated with rich tapestries that depict constellations, maps, and a myriad of symbols that mean nothing to me. They are the same symbols I saw etched into the trees in Garyn, runes for some purpose unknown to me. I should have thought to ask about them. Orbs hang suspended in the air, casting soft light. There is nothing holding them in place but magic. I am impressed in spite of myself. A few children run past us, laughing as they chase a kitten. There is no one to yell at them to stop or to slow down. There is no one to prevent them from being children here.

I tune out Obsidian and Bronwyn as they speak. It is clear that they work closely together, and I wonder just how many people are in the inner-circle of the Empress. More than anything, I just want to see my sister. I am longing to be with someone I know, and who knows me. Someone in whom I find comfort. I am tired of being shuffled between strangers' hands. The children who ran past us just a moment ago remind me so much of Aleca and me when we were little. We spent so many days playing in the fields and keeping going until we fell asleep on the spot. More than once, we woke up to our parents carrying us home. I wish I could go back to that time, to those carefree girls, and tell them to hold onto that for as long as they can.

I do not realize that I am being spoken to until I feel a heavy hand clamp down on my shoulder. With a start, I look up to see Obsidian staring at me.

"I'm sorry, what?" I ask. "I was…distracted."

"I asked you if you were ready to meet with the Empress and to see your sister once more," Obsidian says. My heart leaps and I have to contain my sudden giddiness.

"Yes," I manage to say.

"When you meet with the Empress, it is customary not to look at her until she invites you to do so," Obsidian says. "Be sure to wait until she speaks to you."

"Yes, sir," I say with a nod. He smiles and gives me another clap on the shoulder, and then pushes open the gilded doors before me.

…… † ……

I keep my eyes trained on the floor as we make our way toward the center of the room. Obsidian comes to a halt and quarter-turns to the left. On my other side, I feel Bronwyn do the same, and I copy her.

"Obsidian, thank you," a voice says. It is the most soothing voice I have ever heard in my life, as if wrapping oneself in a blanket. "And Bronwyn….you have served me well in bringing Warrior Grimme to us. I thank you as well. Both of you may leave. I feel Warrior Grimme and I have much to discuss."

"Yes, Empress," they say together. After a moment, the door snaps shut and I am left alone before the Empress. I continue to stare determinedly at the ground, my hands balled into nervous fists at my side. I can feel the sweat forming in them. She does not speak, and I chance a glance up through my eyelashes. All that I am able to see is the deepest blues of her cloak—or is it a dress? Silver stars and moons are embroidered into the fabric, like looking deep into a galaxy. It is exquisite.

"Jace," she finally says. "You may look up." Slowly, I bring my head up and lock eyes with the Empress. She looks more like a goddess than an Empress, and I gasp in spite of myself. Her skin is so dark that it is almost midnight-blue-black. Her eyes, in contrast, are a pure turquoise color. Her hair is a series of elaborate braids and is woven into a crown of crystal quartz.

"Your…majesty?" I greet unsurely. I feel my face turn pink.

"Imperial Majesty," she corrects gently. "But here, you may call me by name. I am Syiera Luna, Empress of Apaiji. We have been waiting for some time to meet you."

"We?" I ask. I cannot keep the hope out of my voice.

"We," she repeats. She motions her arm forward, and Aleca appears from behind her.

"Aleca!" I shout. I run toward her, forgetting myself completely. She runs as well, and we crash into each other in a tight hug. "Oh, Aleca! I have missed you so much. I'm sorry,

I'm so sorry!" I am vaguely aware that I am crying, but I am unable to stop myself. The last time I saw Aleca, she was locked in a solitary cell.

"I've missed you too, Jace! I've been trying to find you for weeks, to contact you," she tells me. We pull apart, both of us wiping at our eyes. "You've cut your hair!" she exclaims, reaching out and touching my short strands.

"What have you done with yours?" I gasp, also reaching out. Her normally-silver strands have been dyed a mixture of blue, indigo, and purple. Her hair curls gently, and boasts a crescent moon and crystal dewdrops fixed into it. I take a step back and examine Aleca. She is clad in a blue and bronze one-shouldered dress and wears an armband of feathers on her right bicep. If it weren't for her eyes, I wouldn't even recognize her as my sister.

"Oh Jace, you won't even believe when I tell you—Syiera has made me her apprentice!" Aleca is brimming with excitement, and she clutches at my hands tightly. "What do you think of that?" I look over Aleca's shoulder at Syiera.

"What does that mean?" I ask her.

"Your sister is training under me. She is most accomplished in the ways of magic, particularly for someone who was raised so far from it," Syiera says.

"And Bronwyn has been helping me See!" Aleca cuts in. "I've been watching for you, but you were so hard to See. Bronwyn says that it is because you are too guarded. I've seen

Battlewood, though! Oh, Jace, it's terrible there," she says. "Commander Raznik has been up to something. I saw…" She trails off, glancing back at Syiera. Syiera nods encouragingly at her, and she turns back to me. "Raznik is hiding something in his walls. Something he does not understand. He is driving himself mad with obsession. I think it has something to do with us…and our parents." My eyebrows snap together.

"Wait a moment, back up. You've been practicing magic, and fortune-telling? You've been using magic to spy on Battlewood?" I cannot wrap my head around it. To see Willow whispering words and handing me stones was one thing, but this…this is entirely different. Aleca is living in the heart of the lifestyle that condemned her to death. "Aleca…you need to show Raznik you have changed, if you want to live freely!"

"We're already fighting about this again? I won't lie about who I am, Jace," Aleca says with a frown. "This is my life! This is what I was meant to do! Training under the Empress! Who could have ever predicted this?"

"I'm sure Bronwyn did," I mutter irritably. I have to get Aleca home, if only for a moment, to placate Raznik. I have no intention of handing my sister over like fresh meat to a rabid animal—I never did—but I cannot live my life in continual fear that someone will find us and kill us. I cannot ask my sister to do that, either. Thinking fast, I say, "What if we could take this back to Raznik and show him that things are not as he has been taught to believe?"

Aleca tosses her hair over her shoulder dismissively. She crosses over the room to a large bowl of water. With one finger, she beckons me over and I begrudgingly join her. With a muttered word, she drags her fingers through the water, drawing a symbol on its surface. With a frown, she tries again, but nothing happens.

"Allow me," Syiera offers. I jump—I did not hear her approach—and move out of her way. Syiera holds her hands above the water, then, eyes closed, she draws the same symbol that Aleca attempted. Instantly, the surface of the water changes, and I am staring into Raznik's quarters. He paces in front of two pictures that have been stuck to the wall. I recognize the people depicted instantly: the faces are mine and Aleca's. Raznik mutters to himself and it sounds like gibberish. Then, without warning, he hurls a knife at each picture. The image in the water disappears, and I am left staring at my reflection.

None of us speak for a few moments. I cannot shake the vision I just watched—nor can I shake the fact that I used magic to see into a different part of the world. There is so much about this world that I do not understand, and I feel more and more lost each day. When I was in Battlewood, I knew my life. I knew my future. Now, I know nothing. I know less than nothing.

"We have to go back, Al," I whisper finally. "I'm not going to ask you to stay there, but we have to go back. We need answers."

EIGHT

I am walking alone with Syiera. She has taken me on a private tour of her gardens and pavilion. The flora that she has so dedicatedly cultivated is a sight to behold. There are plants from all over the world, she tells me. The magic helps to keep them all thriving. She takes me through the citadel and into her private quarters where Aleca has also taken up residence. I can tell instantly where Aleca's space is. She blows through a space like a storm, weaving a path of destruction in her wake. It was always a joke with my family—if you wanted to find Aleca, just follow the trail of paper, books, and toys that she left behind.

She has blossomed into someone altogether different from the shy, shrinking violet she was in Battlewood. I can see the way she has grown into herself, into her confidence. There is a large part of me that wishes we could just stay here forever, without having to venture back to Battlewood. However, I know that Raznik would make good on his promise to send someone after us to kill us. For all I know, he has already sent someone to find us.

"Sit with me for a moment, Jace," Syiera says, motioning to a bench tucked between large palm fronds. We sit in silence, both staring out toward the setting sun. It has only just begun its descent behind the clouds, turning the sky a dusty pink and pale blue. I fiddle with the loose-hanging chains on the bodice of my dress, unsure what else to do.

At last, Syiera speaks. "You care very deeply about your sister," she says. "I can see it in the way you look at her."

"Of course I do," I say. "I don't know how much she told you about our past, but we are each all the other has in the world. Or, we were," I amend. "Now I suppose she's all that I have. She has…this." I motion toward the citadel and the city below us.

"She still needs you," Syiera says gently, resting a hand on my arm. "You need each other."

"How am I supposed to take her away from all of this?" I ask. "This is what she has dreamed of for years, and now she has it."

"I cannot presume to speak for you or your sister," Syiera says, "but I can tell you what I would do in your situation, if you would like."

I turn to face her, staring imploringly. "What would you do?"

"I would get the answers I so desperately sought," she tells me. "Your sister is curious by nature. You are discovering the lies you have been fed for so long. There is still so much to uncover, Jace. I should not be telling you so, but there is much that you have yet to find. Your land—your commander—is built upon a bed of lies. Such an unstable foundation can only last for so long before it begins to crumble. Forgive me for speaking against your land, but I need you to know that Battlewood has already started to crumble. There can never be backward motion, Jace, only forward motion."

Syiera rises and the embroidered train of her dress swirls behind her. Her words remind me so much of Klara in her kitchen: "Gentle forward movement." Everyone seems to have learned this lesson but me. Syiera crosses the balcony, pausing when she reaches the archway that leads back inside. Without turning around, she says, "What is it of which you dream, Jace?"

...... † ......

As it turns out, I dream about nightmarish landscapes that always end with hazel eyes and blood. I am less than amiable when Aleca comes enthusiastically knocking at my door. I ignore the knocking until it becomes more persistent, and I fling my door open.

"What?" I ask in annoyance.

Aleca's grimaces. "What's burrowed in your bun today?" Aleca asks me.

"Nothing," I sigh. I take a step back and allow her in. Aleca comes bouncing forward and throws the curtains open.

"You're lying," she says as she fluffs the curtains before

facing me. "You slept poorly and you've been having nightmares."

"Aleca…," I say, trailing off. She shrugs as she preens in the mirror attached to a wall, playing with her brightly-colored locks. Looking at us standing side-by-side, I can hardly see the resemblance between us. It is only her eyes that give our sisterhood away. She is so happy, healthy, and soft whereas I look so hardened and exhausted. There are lines under my eyes where there used to be none, and a permanent frown threatening to emerge at any point.

"You know, a simple Dreamless Elixir could help you with that," she tells me. "I've used it before. It really works." She comes behind me and begins dragging a gold-gilded brush through my hair. "You aren't taking very good care of yourself, Jace," she suddenly scolds me. "You're falling back into your bad habits."

"What are you talking about?" I ask. "I haven't been drinking or—"

"That's not what I mean," she says. "You're so sad. You're hiding away again."

"I'm right here," I say flippantly, trying to change the subject. It does not work. Aleca grabs my shoulders and turns me to face her.

"Jace Marcais Grimme, that is not what I mean, you know it," she says sternly. We stare at each other for a few moments.

Finally, I relent. "When did you become my guardian?" I

mumble. I turn back around and take the brush from Aleca to continue her work. There is considerably less hair to work through, but I do so slowly and diligently anyway.

"When you stopped loving yourself," she says softly. She wraps her arms around me and rests her chin on my shoulder. "I've missed you, Jace."

"I've missed you too, Aleca," I say. I turn my head to kiss her cheek and she lets out a contented sigh.

At Aleca's behest, I dress myself and allow her to drag me around the citadel complex. She seems to know everyone she passes; she stops here and there to chat with them, and they all beam as they speak. I feel a fierce sense of pride, and it mingles with the dread I feel in having to bring her back to Battlewood. Aleca was made for this life. It is not fair that she should have to give it up just because of archaic laws that have served no other purpose than to oppress us. I do not know what it is that Raznik and his predecessors were so eager to hide, but secrets are a poor base upon which to create a court.

We turn to walk down a hallway, and I can tell immediately that it is different from the rest of the citadel. This hallway is dimmer, quieter, and empty except for us. At the end is a plain wooden door and nothing else. I glance sideways at Aleca in confusion and she holds up a hand. She stands before it and draws a symbol in the air. The symbol begins to glow on the door before it swings open and allows us through. Aleca looks back at me with a triumphant grin.

"Not everyone is allowed to use that spell," she tells me. We walk through the door, and it closes behind us immediately. This hallway is warmer and brightly lit by torches. Portraits of women line the hall. Each has been painted against the backdrop of a constellation, and they all stare off into the distance. "Past Empresses," Aleca says. "Apaiji has always been ruled by women." It is an interesting idea, and I wonder what Battlewood would have looked like if we had been run by women. In Battlewood, women are to be seen and not heard, unless they are of use to the Commander.

"Where exactly is it that you're taking me?" I ask as we draw near yet another door. This one is much more ornate and encrusted with jewels.

"We've been invited to speak with Syiera in her gardens," Aleca tells me excitedly. "This is an honor—so few people are invited to be with her there. Can you believe it? Who would have thought that this is where we would end up? I am training under the Empress of Apaiji! And now you're here with me!" She is still chattering excitedly as she knocks on the door. I make a noncommittal sound. I am having a hard time finding the same level of excitement that Aleca has. She has always managed to look on the bright side of things—almost to a fault. With great effort, I plaster on a smile as the door swings open.

"The Sisters Grimme," Obsidian greets us in his deep voice. He smiles warmly at us and I am shocked to see Aleca's cheeks turn pink. I make a note to keep an eye on this. "We are convened in the garden," he says as we enter. He guides us through a cavernous room. In the very center, there is a dragon carved out of stone. Its wings are open and curve down covetously, hugging a roaring fire in the middle of it. The dragon's mouth is angled upward and opened to allow the smoke out. It is an impressive sight. For a moment, I swear that I can see colorful images dancing in the smoke, but they twist and disappear before I can make sense of them. I draw closer to the fire without realizing I am doing so, and crouch to stare more intently at the flames. This time, I know I am not imagining things: tiny puffs of purples, blues, and pinks all twist around one another in an intricate dance. I still cannot make sense of them, though.

"What is it that you see?" a voice questions from behind me. I leap up and turn around quickly, clasping my hands behind my back. Bronwyn stands before me; she tilts her head to the side as she waits for my answer.

"Nothing, really," I shrug. "Just some colors."

"That was how it started for your sister, too," she tells me. Beside her, Aleca nods her head voraciously. "Colors give way to shapes and pictures, when you are ready to see them."

"It was nothing," I repeat flatly. "We shouldn't keep Syiera waiting." I march ahead of the three of them toward the garden. As soon as I am through the doors and into the patio, I come to a halt. In the center of the garden— even more majestic than the one from the night before— stands a wrought iron gazebo with ivy and flowers crawling up and around it. A pond with a floating globe of falling water is carved into the ground to the right of the gazebo; lily pads rest on the water, their blossoms open to the sun. A myriad of rainbow flowers overflow from all sides. A massive tree stands above the entire area, its branches stretching high and far across the way. White blossoms drip from the branches and coat the ground in a dusting of their delicate petals. Like everything else in this citadel, crystals hang from the tree and glint in the light. I stare in awe at the scene before me.

"It's beautiful, isn't it?" Obsidian asks as he comes to stand beside me.

"I've had dreams about this place…," I say faintly, still looking around the garden. "No, that's impossible," I say, shaking my head. Aleca comes up to stand on my other side, sliding an arm around my waist and resting her head on my shoulder.

"Mother and Father were sitting at the gazebo with Syiera," she says. "I've dreamt it too." I shake my head again as if I can shake off everything that has happened. How can I dream about somewhere I've never been?

"It surprises me that you would say anything is impossible by now," Bronwyn says mildly. "You have seen so much." I let out a humorless snort of laughter as we are guided to the gazebo where Syiera lounges in a gauzy silver gown.

"Empress Luna," Obsidian greets with a bow. We all follow suit and bow as well.

"Obsidian," she greets back. "Ladies, welcome. Please take a seat." She motions to the plush benches around her, the bangles on her wrist ringing as they move. Obsidian and Bronwyn bow again and then walk away, leaving Aleca and me alone with Syiera.

"Thank you for inviting us to your gardens," I say. "It's beautiful here." Syiera raises a hand and a woman appears by her side holding a tray of drinks. We each take one and the woman disappears again. I swirl the beverage around in its glass flute, watching the teal liquid shimmer in the light, before taking a hesitant sip. It is surprisingly floral, almost like lavender.

"May I ask you a question, Empress Luna?" Aleca asks. She plays with the flute in her hand, drink untouched.

"You may," Syiera allows. Aleca spares a nervous glance in my direction before speaking.

"Well…Jace and I have dreamt about this place before…" She trails off as she fiddles with the fabric of her garment. "About our parents being here with you…"

I can see Aleca beginning to lose her resolve and I cut in. "Did it really happen?" I ask.

Syiera sets her flute on the glass table in front of her with a contemplative sigh. Instead of answering, she rises and turns around to lean on the gazebo railing. Aleca and I stare at

Syiera's back expectantly. I am unaware that I am bouncing my leg anxiously until Aleca nudges me with her elbow.

After several moments of silence, Syiera speaks. "I did once know your mother and father," she says slowly. "It was after you were born to them, Aleca, that I first met them."

"Why were our parents here? How did you meet them? When was the last time you saw them?" I do not know what to do with this new information, and it shatters the image of my parents that I have held for so long.

"You are both so much like your parents," Syiera tells us after a very long pause. "You favor your mother, Jace. And, Aleca...you are so very like your father. They were dear friends of mine for some time. I was so sorry to hear of their deaths.

"You must understand that the Raznik dynasty lives in fear of losing their control. The moment they took over, one hundred years prior, they banned anything that could be considered a threat to them. They believed that by ending communication and trade with the outside courts, they could shelter themselves away. Magic was the first thing to go. Those who practiced magic were put to death, and many more of your people fled or went into hiding. The thing about magic, the thing that the Razniks did not believe, was that magic cannot be quelled. Aleca, you are evidence of this.

"The Council of Elders would come together once every ten years or so to try to create a resolution and bring an end to the Pact of Silence. Your Commander elected not to attend these, which meant someone went in his stead. Your mother was his stand-in; we met at one such meeting, fifteen years ago, in Garyn. The moment Aleida and I met, our lives became intertwined. Aleida and I communicated in secret many times over the course of a few weeks, and your father became an integral piece to this. His magic is what fills your veins."

"Our father practiced magic?" we both blurt out at the same time. Syiera smiles indulgently at us before continuing her tale.

"Your father allowed for face-to-face contact by creating a spell that allowed us to communicate through any form of liquid. We had numerous conversations held within a tin coffee mug. It made sense: a warrior needs energy to perform, and thus would carry coffee with them at all possible times. In doing so, I was able to see in real-time what your government was teaching—and hiding.

"The first and only time your parents came to see me, they were planning on uprooting and fleeing with you to Apaiji. I will never know how Commander Raznik discovered this, but he did. In his desperate ploy to maintain his control, he acted out. My girls, your parents did not die because of injury and illness. Your parents were felled at the orders of your Commander."

Her words hang heavy and oppressive in the silence that follows. Neither Aleca nor I make any movement. I do not trust myself to. It is taking every single ounce of self-control to remain where I sit. Blood rushes into my ears, pounding. I feel angry heat flood my face. My hands itch to destroy something, anything, and I hurl my glass of floral drink at the wall of the gazebo. It shatters into a hundred shards that fall to the floor with a tinkling sound. Teal liquid drips down the wall, and I replace it in my mind with Raznik's blood.

"He can't have…" Aleca trails off. "Is that why he wants me dead? Not because I broke the law, but because I have magic?"

"Yes," Syiera says. "Which brings me to my main reason for requesting your presence here today: you must leave us by the next full moon. Both of you." Syiera fixes her gaze on Aleca, who jumps up indignantly. My stomach flops uncomfortably. I knew that our time here was limited, but I was not expecting it to come so soon. The next full moon is only three days away. I do not know if I can face Raznik so soon after discovering that he killed our parents. I do not know if I can ever face him again without attempting to kill him.

"What? No! I can't leave! I won't! Especially not now!" Aleca cries. Her eyes have filled with tears that spill down her cheeks, unchecked.

"You must," Syiera says gently. "If only for a short time. There are answers you seek that can only be found in the land where you once lived. All is not as it seems there; I am sure you understand this, Aleca."

"But…but I…" She protests weakly before falling silent and hanging her head. I chew on my lip unhappily. My leg has taken back up its frenetic bounce. "As you command, Imperial

Majesty," she finally whispers.

"Nothing is permanent," Syiera tells her, "that was the first lesson I ever taught you. But there are lessons that I cannot teach you. Lessons you can only learn on your own," she finishes.

"Something back home," I supplement hesitantly. "But what?"

The Empress fixes a steady gaze on the two of us as she weighs her words carefully. "I have been blessed with a great deal of knowledge—both of things passed, and things yet to come. This knowledge does not come without cost; it is a trying thing to know what I do and to be unable to share it with those who need it most. You must learn for yourselves. Learn from the land you have come from. Discover how you will move forward."

"But Battlewood is not my home," Aleca says quietly. I can hear her fighting to keep her voice steady. She turns away with a tiny sniffle. "May I be excused from your gardens?" Syiera nods and I watch Aleca as she walks down the steps and into the citadel, dejected. She joins Bronwyn and Obsidian just inside the room with the dragon fire pit, and I watch them as they speak in low voices together.

"Is she welcome back?" I ask, still staring after her. "When all of this is over? Please don't punish her for my mistakes." I turn to face Syiera, imploring.

"She is always welcome here," Syiera says, "as are you. You

must leave by the week's close, if only to get this done and over with. Aleca is upset but she will understand in time. She and I have kept a close eye on Battlewood. There is chaos brewing and so much left for you to learn."

I nod absently as I tug on my lip. "We will come back," I tell her.

Syiera smiles at me and rests her hand on my shoulder. "Of that, I am sure," she says.

I welcome the night's arrival. It has been a stressful day and I am more than ready to sleep. Aleca never did resurface; I assume she was nursing her wounds in private. Truthfully, I am not ready to part from Apaiji either. I like it here, despite the cryptic discussions and strange magic. I think I could picture making a comfortable life here, if given the chance. I doubt I will ever fully be comfortable with magic, though.

At last, I am ready to sleep. I move to extinguish my fire, and then pause. Although I know I am alone, I glance furtively over my shoulder before turning back to face the fire. I stare at it for any sign of color or imagery like I saw earlier.

"Show me Willow," I whisper to the crackling flames. They dance merrily in the hearth but show me nothing. Feeling foolish, I pour water from a pitcher onto the fire and watch the hearth go dark. I am about to snuff my candle and clamber into bed when there is an insistent tapping at my window. I yank the curtains open, ready to scold whoever is tapping the glass. There is a pitch-black raven with a letter tied to its leg. I recognize the bird instantly and reach for the letter with trembling fingers. The raven takes flight the moment I have relieved it of its burden.

I perch at the edge of the bed and open the letter. Raznik's angry words fill the page.

"Grimme,
I grow weary of waiting. Have you forgotten what you were sent to do? Do not fail me, Grimme. I will find you, no matter where you run. The choice is yours to make, but I would suggest you make it soon.
Commander
P.S., It may interest you to know that I met your little friend from Garyn. She was most loyal to you, right up until the end. I have sent you a souvenir to remember her by."

I feel my stomach coil as I read his words. I tip the envelope upside down until something soft drops into my hand. I let the letter and the envelope fall to the ground in horror as I recognize what he has sent me. I have to press my hand to my mouth to stop myself from screaming. One perfect copper curl rests in my palm, tied tightly with a thin black ribbon. Beside it rests a finger, thin and perfectly preserved. As soon as I touch it, it turns to dust and disappears, leaving behind the lock of hair.

He has killed Willow.

...... † ......

"Get up," I say, shaking Aleca roughly. She grumbles and tries to pull her covers over her head. "Aleca, get up. Now!" I rip the covers off of her and start gathering her clothes into a bag.

"Jace, what are you doing?" she asks me. She sits up and rubs her eyes as she watches me. "What happened?"

"We're going back to Battlewood now. Don't argue with me, Aleca. I'm your big sister. Get up, get dressed, and meet me outside in ten minutes." I throw the half-filled pack at her and then storm down the hallway toward the entrance of the citadel.

My entire body is shaking with rage and despair. Several times, I have to crouch in the hall to gather my wits. All I can concentrate on is the red rage that has twisted itself around my body. Willow is dead because of me, another mark in my ledger. Another person dead because they dared to get close to me. I force myself to rise and continue moving.

I pace outside of the citadel for what seems like an eternity before I hear the doors open.

"Finally!" I snarl, whipping around. "What the hell—oh, Empress Luna!" I straighten immediately and clasp my hands behind my back.

"What has happened?" she asks me as she hurries down the steps, Aleca in tow. "Your sister came to find me and could give me no detail." Her face wrinkles with concern.

"Raznik has gone too far," I say stiffly. "Again." I hand her the crumpled letter and watch her press her lips together as she reads. "He sent me a lock of her hair and a finger," I tell her. My voice quavers and I will myself not to cry. Now is not the time to allow my emotions to get the better of me. I need to keep my resolve firm.

"Who is 'her'?" Aleca asks me.

"The finger disappeared almost immediately, though." I do not answer Aleca.

"What do you mean by disappeared?" Syiera asks sharply.

"It turned to dust as soon as I touched it," I say. Behind Syiera, I see Aleca gag. Syiera's eyes lock onto me, sharp and scrutinizing.

"So the rumors are true, then…" Syiera muses to herself. "Come with me." She turns and begins to walk back toward the citadel. Aleca starts to follow her, but I do not move.

"We're leaving," I say, crossing my arms. "Now."

"You are welcome to leave, Jace," Syiera says, "but not before I show you what needs to be seen." Her tone is gentle, but I am aware that it is a command. I grind my teeth together before following Syiera. She leads us back into the room where Aleca and I first reunited. Syiera heads straight to the scrying bowl but holds a hand up to stop Aleca and me from joining her. We stay back but watch Syiera closely. She murmurs to herself over and over as she examines the images in the water.

Eventually, she beckons us over to see what she sees. I cannot make much sense of it. It appears mostly in blurry, watery shapes that warp with the ripples of the liquid.

"That's Raznik," Aleca says, her voice hardly above a whisper. "But what is he doing?" I squint harder at the water, trying to see what Aleca is seeing. At last, the images become strong and clear, as if I am standing there with him. I watch as Raznik etches a circle into the ground with an ornate metal staff. I have never seen him carry this staff before. He adds more lines to the image, beads of perspiration forming on his forehead. Once he has finished, he takes a step back to analyze the image. I can hardly decipher what he has drawn but it seems to satisfy him. I do not understand why Syiera has deigned to show us this. I am about to voice my thoughts when Raznik shouts an odd word into the air. The outline on the floor flares to life and illuminates a circle of runes around an intricate mandala. It continues to burn as Raznik paces around it, speaking more of that same language.

"Battle magic," Aleca gasps. "Raznik…"

"That slimy son of a–!" I break off with a growl. I think back to Aleca's letter: We've been lied to, Jace.

Raznik has had magic all this time.

NINE

Syiera has convinced me to remain at the citadel until first light, when the markets open. I have to admit that her logic is sound—it would benefit us to restock our supplies before crossing back through the Nautilus. We take the time to dress and pack properly before Obsidian comes to escort us to Syiera's quarters. At last, just as the sun begins to rise, we are gathered together around the dragon fire pit. Syiera stands with her back to us as we enter. When she turns around, she holds a package wrapped in cloth. A similar cloth bag hangs at her elbow.

"Aleca, Jace," she intones, "your journey back begins now." I hear Aleca sniffle beside me and my stomach drops. How many times will I be the cause of my sister's tears? "Jace, you are to be gifted this." She carefully hands me the cloth-wrapped package. I unwrap it and let out a gasp. A shortsword, sheathed in leather, rests beside a matching leather back holster.

"Oh gods," I whisper, pulling the sword out of its sheath. The blade is unlike any I've seen before, with runes etched down its entire length. It changes colors as it moves in the light: from purple, to green, to blue, and back to purple. Intricate silver wire has been wrapped around the base, holding small gems tightly in the shape of a crescent moon. Pressed into a resin globe at the edge of the base is a bright purple moonflower. "I can't accept this, Syiera. This is…"

"A gift from the goddess Karishua herself," Syiera says. "A blade made of diamond and a straight shot to any target. I would not advise turning down a gift from any god or goddess. This is the path you have walked alone for so long. Let yourself be guided. You will know when you need this."

"Thank you," I say with a bow. I immediately fix the holster around my shoulders and tuck the blade inside. The weight against my shoulder blades is a comforting ally. Syiera nods to me before turning her attention on Aleca. She pulls the bag off of her arm and gives it to her.

"Aleca, this is for you. You have found favor with me and my spirit guide. While you are away, continue your lessons."

Aleca takes the bag and roots through it. Her eyes light up as she takes stock of its contents. I can hear glass bottles clinking together from inside the bag, and she clutches it tightly to her chest.

"Thank you so much, Empress!" she says. "And thank your guide for me," she adds. "I'll use this well."

"I do not have doubts about either of you. I know you will choose well, no matter what happens." Syiera fixes her gaze on me, and I hear the unspoken words. This is your chance to find out who you are. "I shall have Obsidian guide you to the city. From there, you will continue on alone. Safe travels, and may the goddess be with you."

Obsidian meets us outside of Syiera's quarters and we follow him quietly. I half-suspect that Syiera has sent him with us to prevent Aleca from giving me the slip before we can even begin our journey home. He leaves us at the entry to the city with a deep bow.

"Take care of yourselves, sisters Grimme," he tells us. We exchange a firm handshake before Aleca flings her arms around him.

"I will miss you, Obsidian," she says. I narrow my eyes as I watch the two hug.

"And you, Aleca," he says. "Protect yourself."

"I will," she promises. They break apart and I grab hold of Obsidian's forearm tightly.

"She is only a child," I tell him in a warning tone. I will not have Aleca fall into the hands of a grown man, despite her affections toward him. He understands my words immediately and nods.

"I mean nothing more than friendship, Jace," he assures me. "I have told her that my preoccupations lie…elsewhere, at any rate."

"Good," I say, nodding curtly and clapping a hand on his upper arm. "You're a good man, Obsidian. Thank you for caring for my sister." We nod at each other once more, and then part ways.

The city is awake and bustling by the time we make our way from the citadel. Syiera has provided us with money to replenish supplies, with some to spare. It is another reminder of how much of what we have been taught is a lie. Aleca continues to pester me about whose hair and finger Raznik sent to me, but I will not answer her questions. It is a game that she has always tried to play, trying to annoy me into answering, but I do not crack. Eventually, with a huffy sigh, she gives up.

We stop first at a weaponry shop. Aleca's discomfort is obvious, and I make an apologetic noise as I tug her along. I need to get new polish and my dagger could stand a good sharpening. Before he starts on the dagger, the shopkeeper offers to take my sword as well. I shake my head. Something tells me that nothing could weaken that weapon. I look around as the shopkeeper works. I find two wrist sheaths with miniscule blades tucked into them and I call Aleca over. She protests before I can even speak.

"No, I don't want weapons," she says. "I don't like them."

"I'm not saying that you have to use them," I tell her, "but you need to be prepared. You may have made it through unscathed the first time, but luck can only stay on your side for so long. Please, Al?" I plead. "I'll show you how to use them…you could use them for cutting herbs, you know. Gathering magic supplies? It doesn't just have to be for defense." I can see her resolve weaken as she stares at the thin wrist bands; the allure of anything magical is too much for her to withstand.

"Fine," she relents, "but that means I get to choose something for you, too."

"You don't know the first thing about weapons," I begin.

"No, not here," she cuts in, "from a different shop." I shrug—what harm could it do? Compromise reached, I ask for the sheaths to be added to the bill.

The shopkeeper hands me my dagger back with a warning. "This blade has a darkness to it," he says. "Do not let it overtake you." He says nothing else and I take it carefully.

"Thank you," I say, securing it to my hip. He nods and turns away, busying himself again. "Though I doubt that's true…," I add in a mutter. I help Aleca don her new wrist sheaths and we continue on. I can see her tugging at them in my peripheral vision. She'll get used to them eventually. I refuse to allow my sister to go into the thick of things unprotected.

There are several shopfronts and kiosks selling fruits, vegetables, and dried foods for trips. I purchase some and a bag to carry them in, plus two new water skeins. My old belongings have all certainly seen better days. Not a single thing I own is without tears, marks, or holes. Aleca and I allow ourselves the luxury of a new set of clothing each for travelling. The boots will give me blisters before they are broken in, but they are built to last and I need something of substance.

We make one more stop before we reach the sea. The dusty old shop looks like it has been standing here since the dawn of time. Its wooden sign is warped and fading as it swings in the breeze. Though the windows are large and open, a tapestry hangs to prevent outsiders from seeing in. It looks shady to me, but Aleca strides toward it with confidence. A bell rings as she pushes the door open.

"Diviner Eloway?" she calls. "It's Aleca!" The door shuts and there is no light save for two misshapen, melted candles burning on a desk. I squint in the darkness. "This won't do," Aleca murmurs. She cups her hand in front of her and whispers into it. Without warning, a purple flame ignites in her palm. I give a shout and jump backward, knocking over a heavy book in the process.

"You…your hand…"

"Yes, I think that's much better," she says with satisfaction. "Come on. She must be out back." After another look around, Aleca jerks her head toward the back of the shop. The shelves are overflowing with books, and more are piled all over the floor as well. On random displays here and there, wooden boxes holding cards and jewelry are laid out. Aleca forges through the store with ease. I, on the other hand, manage to knock something over at every turn. "Really, Jace," she chides me, "aren't you supposed to be the one who can navigate without issue?" I steady a precariously wobbling stack of books with a grimace.

"Just keep moving," I tell her. We pass through another tapestry and my eyes water at the sudden burst of light. I look around as they adjust, taking stock of my surroundings. This room is bright and airy, the exact opposite of the shop we were just in. Flowers hang upside down in bunches, drying in the sun. An old woman is hunched over a fire. We draw closer and I see she is stirring something in a large pewter cauldron. She throws a few herbs and a stone into the mix and stirs again.

"Diviner Eloway," Aleca says again. The woman turns around and looks in Aleca's direction. Her eyes are a milky blue and I realize she is blind.

"Apprentice Grimme," she says in a soft, nearly whispery voice. She breaks into a toothless smile. She takes Aleca's hands in her own withered ones and kisses them. "Who is with you?"

"My sister, Jace. I have told you about her," Aleca says. "Jace, this is Diviner Eloway. She is the one who has been teaching me all about divination. She's the Divining Master in Apaiji."

"Hands," Diviner Eloway says. She holds her hands out expectantly and I reluctantly give her mine, shooting Aleca a skeptical look. "The hands of a warrior," she says, running a finger along my callouses, "hard-fought battles...love lost…fear underneath a hard exterior…a desire to prove yourself. You have walked a hard road. You make things harder on yourself than they need to be. Your battle is not over, young warrior, but it will be." She lets me go and I wipe my hands on my pant legs uncomfortably.

"Diviner Eloway, I was wondering if you had anything that might benefit Jace. You know, some form of protection, or…or something," Aleca finishes unsurely.

"No more stones," I cut in. "I have more than I know what to do with by now."

"No stones," Diviner Eloway agrees. "You need something stronger." She thinks for a moment and then nods. "A sigil, perhaps. Come here, child." She walks toward a table laden with needles, quills, and pots of ink. She feels her way around the table until her hand comes to rest on a wooden bar. "Well what are you waiting for?" she demands. "Come over here."

Aleca gives me a push toward the old woman. Grumbling, I join Diviner Eloway by the table. Without asking, she grabs my left arm and pushes up the sleeve of my tunic. She dips a needle into a pot of golden ink and then steadies the needle above my flesh. I cannot even open my mouth to protest before she brings the wooden bar down on the needle. I watch helplessly as the blind woman tattoos my skin. She exudes power in a way that renders me useless in the face of it. I cast a look of desperation over my shoulder at Aleca. She flashes a grin back at me and shows me a mark on the inside of her wrist.

After several minutes of silent work, Diviner Eloway sets the needle and bar aside. "Aha," she says. She places a hand above the fresh mark, nearly touching it. It flares a bright, brilliant gold once and then the pain and redness recede. I stare at the mark in an attempt to make sense of it. It feels as if I have seen this image before, but I am unable to place where.

"Thank…you…?" I struggle. She claps her hands with a nod. "What is this?"

"I do not know," Diviner Eloway says with a shrug. "But you will, in time."

I gape at her, incredulous. "You tattooed something on me and you don't even know what it is?"

"I am never misguided," Diviner Eloway informs me with a pat on my cheek. "Diviner Eloway is never misguided."

...... † ......

Talolyn is waiting for us at the dock when we finally arrive. He flashes us a grin and I find comfort in the old man. He may be eccentric, but he is a friendly face in a trying time. We are guided to our onboard sleeping quarters and then left to our own devices. Having not slept the night before, I lay down for some time and attempt to calm my mind enough to rest my body. I have been running on pure spite and adrenaline and it has begun to catch up with me.

When I awaken again, the room is empty. I shake myself from the twisted blanket and out onto the deck. Aleca is at the bow of the ship, clutching her stomach. She glances up at me as I come to stand beside her and lets out a groan.

"I really wasn't planning on being back on a ship anytime soon." She moans as the ship bobs in the water. "Or ever."

"I know," I agree. "Try this." I hand her a sprig of peppermint to nibble. It was a tip that I learned quickly into my warrior training—sailing the waters of Battlewood in the winter makes for precarious and treacherous travel, and the waves toss the ships as if they are toys. I made sure to stock up when we left Apaiji.

"Thanks." She takes the sprig with shaky fingers.

I lean over the railing and stare at the waters below us. I wish that I could see into them the way that Syiera and Aleca can. What is happening in Battlewood? How is Willow's village coping without her? I know that my reaction—anger and a renewed thirst for vengeance—will not be in keeping with Garyn's philosophies. Though I hardly think that they will be prepared to forgive Raznik, either. There is so much that I still do not know about Garyn. I wish I had asked more questions. I wish I had taken advantage of my time there. I wish that I understood why Raznik, so against the use of magic and anything to do with it, has lied to us all this time. I cannot stop thinking about the image Syiera showed us. I cannot get the image of Raznik casting a circle of runes out of my head. All this time, he has had—and used—magic, while putting others to death for the very same thing.

And now I have discovered that my parents were involved in

this too. I am more acutely aware than ever that they are dead. There are so many unanswered questions. There are so many lies we have been fed; how do we even start to sift through these and find the truth? What else has been hidden from us? Nothing I have been told has proven to be remotely true. To top it all, despite Raznik's best efforts to quell magic, Aleca is proof that it cannot be contained. I can feel my head spinning: my thoughts are shooting in a hundred directions at once.

"What do you think we're going to go back to?" Aleca asks me. She is still nibbling delicately on the peppermint, but the color has begun to return to her face. "I mean, I've seen what it's been like over the last few months. It isn't good, Jace. Battlewood is falling apart. Raznik is seriously unhinged. And magical. That's—"

"—a hideous combination, yeah."

For a while, the only sounds between us are the waves on the side of the ship and the birds calling to one another.

"You know," Aleca finally says, "when I was little, I used to dream about where we would be when we were older. Everything seemed within our reach. I never dreamed we would be unwelcome in Battlewood." Her voice has become a whisper. "Sometimes I wonder what it would have been like if we had been born somewhere else."

I glance over at her. She has grown in the past few months. She is taller than I am, though lanky while I am muscular. And she is more confident than before. But, in spite of that, I still see the vulnerable little sister whom I've always tried to protect. It is in moments such as these that I am so aware that Aleca is still a child in many ways.

"It doesn't matter where we come from," I tell her as I sling an arm around her shoulders. "What matters is where we go from here." She rests her head against my shoulder and we fall into silence, watching the water sparkle as we sail.

...... † ......

"I can't believe I didn't think about this before!" I say, bursting into Aleca's room. She looks up at me, startled. I wave her journal in front of her face.

"My notes!" she cries. "You found them!"

"I wasn't about to let Raznik get them, was I?" I leaf through the pages, scanning what I've written. "We both know so much more than before. Get a quill, and meet me in Talolyn's quarters."

When Aleca joins me, I've already unraveled Talolyn's largest map of the Nautilus. He is a veritable well of knowledge and he talks to me about all of the courts while I sketch a haphazard map inside the notebook.

"Where are you from, Talolyn?" I ask. "It seems like you've been everywhere."

"Aye, I have," he says. "I've been to many a land beyond what yer maps show ye." Talolyn taps his temple with a grin. "This ol' noggin is filled with stories, if ye lasses ever wanny hear 'em."

"Are you from the Nautilus?" Aleca asks. "I've forgotten there are other lands and courts beyond our small corner of the world," she admits.

"It's easy to, when you've been raised to believe your court is the only one that matters," I point out. "Even warriors forget, sometimes."

"Yer ol' Talolyn is from a court far from here," Talolyn says. "Maybe someday'll come when ye can join me on a visit."

"We would like that, I think," I say with a nod. I offer a small smile at him, and he claps a hand on my shoulder.

"Now tell ol' Talolyn, lasses, what are ye tryin' to do with a dirty ol' map and some notes?"

Aleca looks at me hesitantly—is it safe to tell him, do you think? I nod almost imperceptibly but she takes enough comfort from that to begin explaining.

"We're trying to find the truth."

Talolyn makes a good audience. He never interrupts Aleca or me as we help each other put the story together. The only time he starts is when we mention our parents, but even then, he does not speak. When at last we finish, Talolyn lets out a low whistle.

"So what happens now?" he asks us. "Are ye really gonny go back to yer homeland?"

"Yes," I say, "we have to. May we look more closely at your map? There may be an easier way to get back than going through Bharasus." In truth, I do not want to go through

Willow's village, though I will never admit that out loud.

"Bharasus?" Aleca asks. "Where is that?"

"Garyn, just past Devent Gorge," I remind her. "How could you have already forgotten that?"

"I didn't go through Bharasus," she tells me, frowning. "I crossed over the Maelos Mountains and into the village of Dezaiyr." I let out a bark of laughter.

"We took opposite routes to get to the same endpoint," I laugh with disbelief. "Of course we did."

"Well, I think that pretty much sums up our relationship," Aleca says. "Same vague goals, completely different ways of achieving them." I shake my head, sobering.

"Your goals were always the nobler of the two." A pregnant pause stretches between us before I turn my attention back to the map. Technically, it is a faster route to take Dezaiyr and hike through Maelos, but that is a volatile land—Maelos has been known to undergo avalanches in the peak of summer. I weigh up the options carefully before speaking.

"I have…acquaintances in Bharasus," I say slowly. "I'm sure you don't need reminding that I'm not a particularly welcomed guest wherever I go. It may be better for our safety to trek back through Willow's– I mean, through Bharasus."

"Who do you know in Garyn?" Aleca asks, eyeing me closely. I wave her question away and focus on the map. I can feel her continue to stare at me as I lean over the table. At last, she drags her gaze back to the map. "I went through a village in

Kydier called Yolchame. They are a safe place."

"I went through there as well, although I'm not sure if I am welcome back," I say, chewing on my lip.

"Why?" Aleca asks. "What happened?"

"Did you meet a man named Bamet?" I pick at the cuticles on my nails as I speak. Aleca makes a sound of disgust.

"Yes. He's an absolute boar," she says. "Did you get into a fight with him or something?"

"Or…or something," I hedge. I look up and lock eyes with Aleca. "I killed him."

"Jace!" she cries, voice reproving.

"In my defense, I gave him the option to walk away," I counter. "Trust me, Aleca, the world is not missing him." She tugs at her lip uncomfortably and I shrug.

"I guess we will have to risk going through Yolchame," she says. "I do not know much about the rest of Kydier, and I don't think this is the time to try to learn."

"Let Talolyn make ye a trail map," Talolyn offers. "I'll bring ye straight to yer endpoint, and give ye advice 'long the way."

"That's very generous, Talolyn," Aleca says.

"Yes, thank you," I agree.

Talolyn shakes out a piece of parchment and begins to draw. Aleca takes the notebook from me and flips through it interestedly. When she gets to Willow's writing, she stops.

"Who wrote this?" she asks me. "Is it the person who Raznik killed? Is that how you know people in Garyn?"

"Do you ever get tired of asking questions?" I snap. "Focus, Al. We need to figure out how we're getting through and back to Battlewood."

"Ye know, I just thought of who ye remind me of," Talolyn pipes in. "Ye and yer sis."

"Yes?"

"Years ago, I sailed a man and a woman. What'd they call themselves, now?" Talolyn strokes his chin as he thinks. "If I ain't mistaken, they were doin' the same thing as ye are. Gatherin' info. Writin' a code. Came through here only once."

"Were their names Jasper and Aleida?" I ask him. His eyes brighten at the names and he gives an enthusiastic nod. "Our parents."

"Syiera was right," Aleca whispers. "Our parents were trying to learn the truth too."

"We're finishing what they started," I say firmly. "Talolyn, what else can you tell us about the lands?"

...... † ......

Another day passes before we finally reach land again. When we do, Aleca stumbles onto the shoreline with a sigh of relief. Talolyn stands at the foot of the ramp while we get our bearings and then hands me a rolled piece of parchment.

"Yer map," he tells me. "Be careful going through Wesbeoun." He points to the spot on the map, marked with a red star. "They're a travellin' commune, known fer strikin' first an' askin' later."

"It was them who did this," I say with a point to my shorn locks. "A trade." Talolyn nods grimly.

"Yer lucky that's all they asked fer." He holds up his left hand, and for the first time, I noticed that his middle finger is missing the top two-thirds. I shake my head in sympathy. "Stick to the map and ye should be fine. I 'spect we'll be seein' each other soon. Fare thee well, lasses." Talolyn turns and strides back up the ramp. For the first time, Aleca and I are well and truly on our own together.

I do not remember what it feels like to have travelled with her. We used to take trips together from our house to the waters and forests near our village. Mother would pack us meals, Father would provide us with paper and drawing materials, and we would go off on our own. When our parents died, I tried to keep up the tradition. I quickly fell away from anything that reminded me of my parents, though, and turned to anything that would numb the loss instead. I would frequently abscond with less-than-reputable peers and leave Aleca to fend for herself. It is something I have come to regret deeply, and I do not think I could ever forgive myself for not being there when Aleca needed someone most. I can only hope that from here on out, I will always be there for her. I cannot make up for what happened in the past, but I can give her the kind of love she deserves now.

We take shelter shortly before the sun begins to set. We have not yet come across Wesbeoun, for which I am grateful. I start a fire while Aleca takes it upon herself to ward our campsite. It is strikingly similar to how this trip began, and I feel a dull ache in my chest. She joins me by my side and pulls out the bag given to her by Syiera.

"May I?" Aleca asks, holding up a shimmering black dust.

"What is it?" I ask.

"It will help See in the flames. I'm curious to see if it affects you. You saw something in Syiera's fire, didn't you?"

"What are you talking about?" I ask dismissively. Aleca fixes me with a stony stare and I relent. "Fine, yes. I just saw colors, though. It was probably the mosaics of the fire pit."

"Just settle in and stare at the flames," Aleca instructs. She waits while I draw my knees to my chest. I drape one arm across them, resting my chin on it, and let my other arm dangle straight in front of me— close enough to the flames that I can feel the fire's heat without being burned. "Ready?"

"Yeah."

With a low-hummed word, Aleca drops the powder into the flames. They flare bright blue before dulling back to their yellow-orange-red. I stare intently into the fire; I don't know what I'm supposed to be looking for, but this seemed important to Aleca. After quite some time, though, she lets out a sigh.

"Well, maybe you're not ready yet," she relents. She moves to pour water on the flames when I throw an arm out to stop her. Staring back at us from the fire is Raznik, teeth bared and eyes wild. In the next moment, he is gone and it is just the flames again. Aleca and I exchange a long stare before she puts the fire out.

"Raznik is spying on us," she breathes. I nod slowly. Nowhere is safe for us now.

after the last fall

TEN

"Are you sure we need to go back?" Aleca asks as we pack our bags and prepare to continue on. "I mean, it's pretty obvious at this point that we're going to be–,"

"I'm not going to let anything happen to you," I cut her off.

"What about you?" she presses. I ignore her as I cinch my bag shut and swing it over my shoulder.

"Are you ready, Al?" I ask.

"You're avoiding my questions again." She crosses her arms over her chest with a frown. I nudge her bags with the tip of my boot and she picks them up, grumbling.

"It's what I do best. Come on."

We make our way steadily across the rocky land, pausing only once to fill our skeins with water. We spend a large portion of the day arguing over whether or not we should walk through Wesbeoun or around it. Aleca has had the fortune of not being seen as an enemy immediately upon arrival. I cannot say the same. Because of this, she does not understand the dangers surrounding an unwelcome entry.

Aleca is smart, but too optimistic by half. She is quick to see the good in everyone and rarely acknowledges the darkness. I, on the other hand, have been trained to see the darkness first and never to take anything at face value. It is a cynical way to live but it has saved my life on more than one occasion. It is the same argument I had with Willow— and look where it landed her. I refuse to allow the same thing to happen to my little sister.

At last, Aleca relents and agrees to remain on the outskirts of Wesbeoun instead of charging through. I know she is not happy about it, but I would rather she be annoyed and alive, than foolhardy and dead. Having dealt with these people, I have no interest in dealing with them again if I do not have to. If we play it carefully, we can bypass the entire village. It will add time to our trip, but it is worth it.

We find a place to settle as night begins to creep across the sky. It is near the border of Wesbeoun, but far enough away that we should remain relatively unseen. Aleca has sworn on her life that her wards will guard us, and I have no choice but to trust her. I have seen for myself that magic is real, and that it is powerful, but I do not like that I have to put my safety at the mercy of an unseen force. Despite Aleca's adamant reassurances, I keep my blade drawn and near me at all times in case I should need it. Aleca has begrudgingly kept her wrist sheaths on. Frankly, she would be useless in a battle, but it makes me feel better to know that she has some form of physical protection.

I can see her dozing by the fire in spite of her attempts to remain awake. I eventually send her to bed, and she does not put up much of an argument. Left to my own devices, I pull my sword closer and stoke the fire. I do not intend to let my guard down this close to the village. I can still hear the woman shouting at me as I left the weapons tent, and I have no doubts that she meant each word. Once I am sure that Aleca has fallen into a deep sleep, I pick up my sword and walk the perimeter of the clearing.

The blade gives off a subtle glow in the darkness, and it is enough for me to see my path without giving me away. I prowl slowly, careful not to make any noise. It is evident that the village is a seasonal one— the permanent buildings are few and far between and outnumbered by thick canvas tents. If my calculations are correct, we are nearing the autumn equinox. The leaves of the trees have only just begun to change colors, but there is a definite chill to the night that was not there only a week ago. A village such as Wesbeoun, will be preparing to pack up and move to warmer climes soon. Not everyone is able to withstand the cold.

I cannot sense any movement from the village, and even their fires are weakly-pulsing embers. With a sigh of relief, I turn away and begin the trek back to camp. I freeze as I see the woman from the weapons tent through an opening in the trees.

I press myself against a trunk, breathing carefully through my mouth. A silver braid trails over her shoulder from beneath her cloth hat; my blood boils at the sight of my hair adorning her body. She seems to be looking for something and is keeping her eyes trained to the ground, only a small lantern providing her light. It would be easy for me to gain the upper hand over her, retribution for my hair. My fingers itch as they grip the handle of my blade and I have to restrain myself from charging her. Instead, I make do with watching her.

She drops to her knees and brushes branches and old leaves aside. I have to press a hand to my mouth to muffle my gasp as she wrenches a door open from the ground she just cleared. I can hear someone shout something indistinguishable as the door opens. As gingerly as possible, I ease closer to the opening to get a better vantage point. She doesn't enter into the doorway but throws a sack down through the opening.

"Shut up!" the woman shouts in her harsh voice. "Be happy with what you've got. You deserve less than that!" No more sounds come from behind the door. Before I can see anything else, the door is slammed shut again. The woman looks around for a moment and then makes her way back to the village. I wait for as long as I can until I feel it is safe enough to investigate the trap door.

It is well and truly dark now; I can barely make out my path ahead of me. For a moment, I wonder if I would be able to conjure light the way that Aleca did in Diviner Eloway's shop.

I wouldn't know where to begin, though. I don't know what she said to make the light appear. Here, though, hidden under the blanket of darkness, I can afford to feel a bit more foolish than I may otherwise allow. I bring my hand to my mouth the way that Aleca did and then pause. What would I even say?

"Light!" I whisper. Nothing happens, and I try again. "Please light?" Nothing. I let out a huff. "Oh, come on. Just guide me here, please! I don't know what I'm doing!"

It seems to have done the trick: soft, silver light fills the palm of my hand. "Holy hell," I whisper, staring at it. "I did that. I did magic." I stare at it for another moment before remembering where I am and what I'm doing. With the assistance of the light, I can make out the door that has been hastily re-hidden by natural debris. I test the ground around it to make sure it is not an actual trap. Confident that I can move forward, I stoop to remove the leaves and I make contact with a rusted circular handle. I do not know whator — who—is in there, but I get the feeling that it is not an enemy. Based on the interaction between the woman and whoever she was talking to, they are not friends. I make sure my sword is ready for the kill, should I need it. With a grunt, I tug the door open and hold out the silver light. There is movement and then I come face-to-face with a pair of familiar hazel eyes and wild copper curls.

The light in my palm extinguishes as I back up on shaking legs. I can feel my eyes wide with disbelief, and her face reflects the same emotion.

"This isn't real," I whisper, squeezing my eyes shut. When I open them again, she's come out of the trap door and is closing the space between us.

"Jace?" she whispers back. She reaches an arm out with tentative fingers that curl around the air. "But they told me you were—"

"— dead?" I finish. "I'm not dead. Not yet."

Willow flings her arms around me in a crushing embrace. I hold her tightly as well, relishing the feeling of her. She rests her chin on top of my head and I can feel her release a shaky breath. When I look up, I realize she is crying.

"I thought…I saw your hair on that awful woman, and she said…but you're…"

"Your hands!" I cry suddenly, grabbing them and examining them frantically. There are no missing fingers; Raznik sent me a proxy. It was all a lie, all a ruse to get me to return. At the thought of Raznik, it suddenly dawns on me that we are still standing in the opening of the forest, easy targets. "Come on," I instruct, grabbing her hand and dragging her after me. She does not put up a fuss.

We make it back to camp without issue, and I relight the fire. I can hear Aleca turning in her sleep, but she does not reappear. By the light of the fire, I can take full stock of Willow. Her hair is tangled with broken branches and dirt streaks across her face. A yellowing bruise creeps down her jawline and onto her neck, and her arms are marred with superficial cuts. Her clothing has definitely seen better days, but overall she seems to be alright. I can feel myself staring at her and have to force myself to look away several times.

There is an awkward silence between us as we sit by the fire. Several times I clear my throat, go to say something, and then change my mind. I'm about to explode from frustration when Willow blurts out, "I'm so sorry, Jace! I never meant to— I shouldn't have— what I mean is, I know why…why you did what you did. I know you were trying to protect me. I've never…I've never needed to be protected like that before. I've never known someone who would protect me like that," she admits. She wipes at her eyes with her fingers. "I shouldn't have let you walk away like that. I went back home instead of going after you, and I regretted every moment of it. It was only after your Commander came into my land that I knew I had to find you."

"Raznik came into your land?" I ask, shocked. "Why? When?"

"It was after I returned," she says, "for a meeting with the Elders. He left angry, and then a few weeks later, we came across each other again. When he intimated that you were to be killed…" She trails off and busies herself by lighting a twig on fire. "I left when the village was asleep. I thought I was doing well on my own. I made it through Garyn and into Kydier with barely a problem. I was planning on stopping to visit Klara and

Romek, but before I could even make it through the ruins, I was captured. They were looking for you, but they found me instead.

"Somehow, they knew we had been travelling together. I have a feeling that your Commander tipped them off; they knew too much about current events in Battlewood to be strangers to the land. They said that if they couldn't find you, I was the next best thing. They blindfolded me and threw me into a caravan. The last thing I could remember was being hit in the back of my head and blacking out. When I came to, I was in their village.

"A woman was talking to them in a foreign language. I couldn't understand what she was saying to them, but I could tell instantly that she was the head of this village. She started asking me all kinds of questions: did I know you, what was I doing across my border, why was I with you? When I told her that we had been travelling together, she took the blindfold off of me.

"'Do you like my hair?' she asked me. 'Took it from your friend. She put up much less of a fight than we expected.' Well, of course, that made me angry, and I started screaming at her. I may have spit at her, to be honest, I was just so mad and upset. Whatever it was that I did, she did not like it. I was blindfolded again and then when I came to, I was in the dark and clearly underground. I think they must have used that place as a prison for people a long time ago; it was obvious it

206

hadn't been used in a while. I wasted a lot of my strength trying to break out of there, and when I realized that I couldn't, I tried to play nice with them. We're not…we're not going through their village, are we?" Her voice has gotten hoarse from talking, and I hand her my skein of water. She drinks from it greedily, not even caring when water spills down her chin.

"Are you insane?" I ask. "We're bypassing it completely." I pull out the map and open it up for her to see the path that Talolyn has drawn for us. She scoots in closer until we are almost touching and looks over the map.

"This is brilliant," she breathes. "Your sister would be thrilled to see this. Wait, your sister! Did you–?"

"Asleep," I say, pointing at the tent.

"One last question: did I see you doing magic?" Willow asks me, mimicking the open palm trick that I managed.

I hand her a piece of dried fruit, a peace offering. "Welcome back," I say, "I have so much to tell you."

...... † ......

"Ahem."

I jolt awake and look around wildly. Aleca stands above me, arms crossed, and an amused look on her face.

"Company?" she asks me, jerking her head at the slumbering Willow resting her head on my shoulder. We must have fallen asleep by the fire at some point in the night. I feel my cheeks turn pink.

"It's…it's kind of a long story," I say sheepishly.

"Is this your 'acquaintance' in Bharasus?" Aleca asks, quirking an eyebrow.

"You ask far too many questions for the morning," I say, stifling a yawn. "Pack the tent, and I'll explain on our way."

Getting past Wesbeoun proves to be harder than we expected. The general village is clustered together, but there are hunters and gatherers that spread out on the fringes. I am anxious to put as much distance as is possible between us and the village— once they realize that their prisoner is gone, there is no telling how they'll react. I don't want Aleca in any more danger than is necessary. It was a lot to ask her to leave Apaiji. I know she misses it, and I know she would much rather be there. Part of me wonders if I ever would have seen Aleca again if I hadn't been sent to retrieve her.

We have made it almost entirely away from Wesbeoun and its surrounding area when we come across a hunter. He is asleep at the base of a tree, weapon held loosely in his hand. My eyes dart around, trying to find the safest and quietest path. I am the only one trained to move silently, and it is not something that comes without a lot of hard work and dedication. Luck is on our side: he is without a hunting dog. He must be a lone hunter, trained by stealth and quick movement. But we will only remain lucky if he stays asleep.

I throw an arm out to stop Aleca as she begins to move forward. Pressing a finger to my lips, I jerk my head in the direction of the man. She nods in understanding and freezes in her tracks. Both of us are well aware that she is not equipped to handle a fight. Even though there are three of us and only one of him, Willow and Aleca are little help to me in a fight.

"What should we do?" Willow whispers to me. I chew on my bottom lip, weighing the options.

"Well," I start slowly, "we could try to pass him without alerting him to our presence—"

"— which you don't think will work," Willow states, matter-of-fact.

"No, I don't," I admit.

"What's our other option?" Aleca asks. She looks between the hunter and me several times.

"We kill him," I say.

"We can't kill him!" Aleca whispers in a panic. "He's…he's unarmed!"

"He's holding a sword," I say with a raised eyebrow. "That doesn't qualify as 'unarmed' to me."

"No, no killing!" she argues. "You said you wanted to prove you had changed! Prove it now! Just…we'll walk really quietly! Watch!" In her haste to change my mind, she begins forward. The first few steps are silent enough, until she steps down on a large, dry branch. It snaps with a ringing crack, and the hunter leaps to his feet in confusion. "Oh gods," she gasps.

"Who's there?" he shouts, looking around wildly. His eyes come to rest on us, and he lets out a triumphant bark. He comes running toward us, and we all stumble backward.

"Oh, nice one, Aleca," I snarl. I pull both my sword and my dagger from their sheaths, prepared to use either one. "Both of you get back and hide!" I shout.

"Where?" Aleca cries. I can hear her panic even more now.

"Climb a tree, I don't know, just GO!" I scream. I don't have time to take care of them and the encroaching threat of harm. The hunter is within arm's reach now, and he lets out a laugh.

"What do we have here?" he asks me. I hold my weapons out, ready to fight, but he makes no lunges at me. "A prisoner and two wanted criminals? Bagging you would bring me more money than I'd know what to do with."

We circle each other, like animals stalking their prey. His eyes flick over my shoulders a few times toward Willow and Aleca. I know he is trying to distract me enough that I'll turn my back on him, but I do not fall for it. He may be a hunter, but he is no warrior. I cannot be fooled by such a basic trick.

"We were kind of hoping you were dead," he says. I feint forward and he stumbles before reclaiming his balance. "It was fun to listen to the redhead cry for you," he continues. "Not that she remembers any of that."

"You're a pig," I say, rushing forward with a swing. I catch his shoulder and he stumbles again with a shout.

"And you're a bitch," he bites back. He tries to cut at my arm, but I swing my offhand with my dagger to block him.

"I've been called much worse," I say with a laugh, "You're

going to have to try harder than that if you're looking to derail me."

We go around for a few more shots before he finally lands a mark. His sword catches in the meat of my thigh muscle and slices down. I let out a string of curses as the fabric of my pants stains red. He laughs and leaps forward again, thinking he has me; instead, I easily move out of his trajectory, and the tip of his blade sticks into the ground. Before he can turn back around, I knock his feet from under him and he goes sprawling.

As soon as he has rolled onto his back, he comes face-to-face with my blade. "I'm going to give you a choice," I tell him. "It's your tongue or your life."

"You're stupid if you think–," he begins furiously.

"I'd think carefully," I say. I press the tip of my sword to his neck just hard enough that a droplet of blood escapes. "See, I could take your life, and be done with it, but I don't really want to do that. But, I can't let you go without collateral, either. How do I know you're not going to run back to your village and tell them what you've seen? I'm not really in the mood to be killed, and I doubt my partners here are either. What is one lone hunter, though?" I fix my gaze on him, raising an eyebrow and smirking.

"Don't kill me," he rasps.

"Get up and follow me," I tell him, kicking his weapon away.

"Did you really cut out his tongue?" Aleca asks me as soon as I return.

"Well, you didn't want me to kill him," I shrug. "So I didn't." She opens her mouth to speak and I hold up a hand to stop her. "No, no more. I am hungry, I am sore, and I want to get the hell away from this place before we have a repeat of what just happened. Get your stuff and move." Instantly, I regret snapping at her. I'll have to make up for it later, but for now, all I can focus on is getting distance between us and Wesbeoun. My leg is screaming its protest as we scale the upward slopes of the land, but I refuse to stop until Willow physically restrains me.

"Will you stop for three seconds so that I can look at your leg?" she asks me, panting. She has wrapped her arms around me tightly from behind, pinning my arms to my side.

"It's just a surface wound, it'll heal," I say, wiggling out of her hold. I can feel my face is red.

"Jace Grimme," she begins sternly, "you—"

"Her middle name is Marcais," Aleca supplements in a whisper.

"Jace Marcais Grimme, you sit down and let me look at that leg right now," Willow demands. I glare at Aleca as I plop myself onto a nearby rock.

"Well, you were being obstinate," Aleca says, tossing her hair over her shoulder unapologetically. "You don't need to try to prove yourself with us. If you're in pain, be in pain. It's not a crime to be yourself."

We both stare at each other as the irony of her words sets it. We are here because we were being ourselves. We are here because Aleca dared to question, and I had to repent for my delinquency.

"Well, maybe I misspoke," she says sheepishly. I laugh at the look on her face and shake my head.

"I need you to move the fabric so I can get a better look at this," Willow says, pinching at my pant leg. It has dried to my leg and sealed itself to the wound. With a grimace, I tear at the fabric above the wound and rip the lower piece off. Pain sears down my leg as the fabric comes free, and I can feel sweat beading my forehead. She pours water onto the spare fabric and carefully wipes around the wound. "Do you still have any of that tincture I gave you?"

"In my bag," I tell her. "It should be in a pouch." Willow rummages through my belongings for a moment before procuring the pouch. When she tips it over and into her palm, the lock of her hair falls with it. She holds it up, staring.

"Is this my hair?" she asks me, brow furrowing.

"Yeah," I say, "courtesy of Raznik. He sent it with your finger—well, not yours, I suppose— and a note to inform me he had killed you. I…may have lost my temper and made Aleca leave with me so that we could go face him once and for all." I look at her briefly and then away with a shrug.

She sets the hair aside and untwists the cap of the tincture.

With gentle fingers, she spreads the tincture across my leg. Almost immediately, the redness begins to dissipate and the cut starts to close. Aleca lets out a gasp and drops to her knees beside Willow.

"How did you do that?" she says. "It just healed like that!" She snaps her fingers.

"She's a healer," I say, "that's her job."

"And how many times has she had to heal you?" Aleca asks with a sly smile.

"I've lost count," Willow says, flashing a sly grin of her own. With a grunt, I heave myself up from the rock and grab a new pair of riding pants to change into.

"Oh good, you're bonding. I'm so glad," I grumble, stomping off behind a bush to change in peace. Their laughter follows me as I go.

······ † ······

I trudge along at the front with Aleca and Willow behind me. I can hear them talking quietly and laughing at times, but I do not join them. I am wrapped almost entirely in thinking about what we will find when we return to Battlewood. I know what I would like to find: a repentant Raznik, a pardon for our actions, our home still there and welcoming. I have a distinct feeling that this is nothing near what I will actually find. If I had to guess, it is more likely that we will cross the border and find ourselves on the sticking end of a sword. Valkyrie Elouned and Commander Raznik were cheated of their conquest once; they will not allow for it to happen again.

I wonder if there is a way that I could keep Aleca and Willow hidden. They think that they know what they are getting themselves into, but I know that they do not. And, just because I am not the same person I used to be, that does not mean when push comes to shove, I won't take someone else's life in order to protect mine or theirs. I rack my mind, trying to remember the blueprints I studied so carefully when I was younger. There are many hidden entrances into Battlewood Castle, and I know that they are not all guarded. I doubt if they are even all known about, to be honest. I learned them so I could sneak around without being caught. My mind kicks into overdrive as I start to reframe my entry plan. Nothing would be more satisfying than to let Raznik think we're coming back on his terms when we are in fact setting the rules ourselves.

By the beginning of sunset, the land has begun to turn more familiar. It is decided that we will set up camp again for the night. Willow and Aleca are worn out, and even I am feeling the effects of the day. The seasonal shift has cooled the temperature, but journeying across constantly changing land under the sun is enough to exhaust anyone. There is a small body of water running nearby, and I send Aleca to fill the skeins. While she is gone, I busy myself by building a fire and pulling out three small soup balls and some dried fruits. I did not realize how hungry I was until we stopped moving but now all that I can concentrate on is the gnawing in my stomach.

I do not feel Willow's presence until she lays a hand on my arm. I look over at her and see that she has her other hand clamped around something. I straighten up and wipe the dirt off of my hands.

"I meant to give this to you before, but I didn't know what Aleca knew, and she has a tendency to ask questions," Willow says. She opens her hand and my amber necklace is nestled in her palm. I take it and hold it up in front of me, looking at it.

"You saved it?" I ask her. I secure it around my neck again and run a finger along the edges of the stone. "Thank you," I add softly.

"I knew I would see you again," she tells me. "I had to see you again." We lock eyes for a minute and then she breaks into a smile. "Besides, clearly you still need the protection to keep yourself out of trouble." Instantly, the heavy mood is broken. I make a face at her and resume preparing our meal.

"I can protect myself just fine," I say with a huff, but there is no bite behind the words. The stone reflects the light from the flames and I run a finger over it again. In spite of all of the terrible things that I have had to deal with in the past few months, there have been bright spots. I just need to learn how to hold on to them.

ELEVEN

I'm woken by a low, distant rumble. I poke my head out of the tent and stare up at the impending storm that threatens to strike at any moment. The sky is a deep, dark grey; the clouds hang heavy and full. We have two options: we can try to outrun the storm, or we can stay here. Either way, we are likely to be caught. We don't stand a chance. The storms are notorious for their violent winds and furious rains. All we can do is remain hunkered down in our tent, though I doubt it will provide us with much protection.

We begin to move once the worst of the storm has passed. The dirt has turned to slick mud and, more than once, we have to help pull each other unstuck as the mud sucks our feet down. The sun remains stubbornly hidden behind the grey clouds and there is a definite chill in the air that was not there before. We have put a large amount of space between us and Wesbeoun, but I still feel the need to look over my shoulder. I cannot shake the feeling that, somehow, we are being watched.

Knowing that Raznik can spy on us makes me uneasy. The fact that he has battle magic is astounding even now. He, more than his predecessors, has been a staunch opponent of magic— of change in general. It was not always a reign of terror under his command. There was a time in which I revered him. After my parents died, and I had become wayward, it was Raznik who pulled me back to my feet and whipped me back into shape. It is because of Raznik that Aleca didn't lose me completely. Trying to compare the Raznik I thought I knew to the Raznik who has emerged makes my head hurt.

Soon, the sky begins to darken again. We have barely gotten our tent set up when the skies open. Rain pelts at the canvas walls viciously, though Aleca has magicked the cloth to repel the worst of it. Unable to light a fire, we tide ourselves over with fruit and jerky. We've been set back a day and it has put us on edge. If it continues to rain like this, the land will become treacherous to cross and we will be stuck. If we are able to make it to Yolchame by tomorrow evening, however, we may be able to move upward and away from the dangerous muds. Assuming they'll allow me re-entry, that is.

At the feeling of something soft hitting my head and bouncing off, I look up and over at Aleca and Willow, who are huddled together on the other side of the tent, giggling. A piece of bread sits in my lap, and I hold it up.

"May I help you?" I ask, dangling the bread between us.

"You always look so intense and serious," Aleca says, imitating my face. She giggles through the furrowed brow, and I roll my eyes, laughing.

"That's because I am intense and serious," I say, tearing a piece off of the bread and rolling it into a ball.

"You're going to get wrinkles if you keep your face like that," Aleca says, "and everyone will say, 'What a pity about that Jace; she used to look so young and beautiful!'"

"Yes, because I am known for my good looks and gentle personality," I say, flicking the balled-up bread at her. "Why did you throw bread at me?"

"We've been trying to talk to you," Willow says, "but there is no reaching you when you're so deep in thought. What were you thinking about?"

"Yolchame," I say. "I don't know if they'll allow me back, considering I killed one of their people."

"Maybe…maybe if you tell them you're sorry…" Aleca trails off.

"I'm not sorry," I say flatly, "and I'd do it again if I had to." Willow and I lock eyes for a moment, and I wonder what she is thinking. Perhaps it sounds cold of me that I so casually killed. I cannot pretend that it was not justified, and I cannot pretend that I regret it. Bamet was nothing but a predator, and I will not allow predators to roam freely.

"They know you killed him," Willow says. "They asked questions, and I had to tell them the truth."

Aleca watches the two of us curiously as we talk. Neither of us has taken our eyes off the other.

"And what exactly is the truth?" she asks us.

"What did they say?" I ask, ignoring Aleca.

"They didn't seem surprised; Klara told me that the commune was discussing exiling him," she tells me. "Bamet is not one of their own, and he was exiled from his own people. They took him in as a mercy."

"Why did you kill him?" Aleca asks more loudly.

"Who were his own people?" I ask. I try to place his features, but they are neutral enough that he could be from anywhere.

"They are a nomad tribe, I'm not sure of their name," Willow responds.

"Excuse me–," Aleca tries again.

"Nomads? Perhaps–,"

"I'm going to start screaming if someone doesn't answer me!" Aleca finally shouts, breaking our trance.

"You are so nosy," I chide her. "It's none of your–"

"Jace saved me from Bamet," Willow cuts me off. "She tried to get me to protect myself, but I didn't listen and I almost lost myself because of it."

"So you're okay with the fact that she killed him?" Her voice is disbelieving, almost betrayed.

"I didn't say that," Willow shakes her head. "But I owe her my life for it."

At last, we break eye contact. It gives me hope to think that I may be welcomed back into Yolchame after all. I enjoyed being around Klara and Romek. They did not expect a complete breakaway from our inherent personalities, despite being strangers. None but Battlewood has. In spite of my eagerness to confront Raznik, I dread returning to Battlewood. How can I, after everything I've seen in the last few months? Though most of my time was spent trudging through the wild, I know that there are so many more cultures and villages in other lands than we've ever been exposed to. If, somehow, I make it through alive, I intend to travel more and learn everything I can. Never again can I live with the blinders that I have had on for so long.

More than that, I know I've only just begun to scratch the surface.

We are up and moving early the next morning. The sky is hazy with leftover storm clouds, but it boasts an empty threat. The sun has already begun to burn through it. As usual, I am the only one who is ready and willing to move. Both Aleca and Willow drag their feet as they walk behind me, and more than once I hear them yawn and stumble. I do not mind the silence— I know that once Aleca has woken up more, she'll do nothing but chatter. Her personality is infectious and draws everyone in. She fits in well with Apaiji, and I will do anything to make sure she gets back there. I don't know how I'm going to get Aleca to Raznik and away again without him killing her, but there must be a way. If she was able to escape from the dungeons, we should be able to get her out of Battlewood once more.

"Aleca," I say suddenly, wheeling around to face her. She and Willow come to a halt.

"Y-y-yeah?" she asks, trying to stifle a yawn.

"How did you break out of solitary when you were supposed to face Raznik?"

"I don't really know," she says slowly. "I had been practicing some basic spells for a while—mostly ones that I made up. Then I got arrested. Some of my spells were for lights and some were for protection from weather, but never anything serious. I guess I was just so desperate to get out and get away that it just kind of…exploded out of me."

"Stress-induced magic," Willow says. "That's probably why you were able to hold light in your hand, Jace. You were scared and emotions give energy. At its root, magic is about intent."

Aleca raises an eyebrow at me. "You did magic, Miss Magic-Is-Fake?" she demands, hands on her hips.

"Obviously magic isn't fake," I say, waving her comment away. "Focus. I'm guessing you've learned how to harness your magic into something a little less…volatile, right?"

"Can I get that in writing?"

"Aleca!"

"Okay, okay, focus. Yes, that's what I've been learning to do under Syiera. Channelling, focusing…"

"How can we use your magic to keep you safe from Raznik?" I ask.

"Is that even possible? Raznik hates magic," she says with a frown. "He'd kill me on the spot."

"Yeah, I'm not really inclined to believe that," I say. "He doesn't hate magic; he hates the idea of losing his power. Battlewood has been under his family's control for nearly a century. It was his great-grandfather who signed the Pact into existence, and his family has ruled since. There is something he is hiding from our people. We've been isolated from other lands for so long that we just accept it as truth but, somehow, that's starting to change. Our parents had something to do with it, and we've become his revenge. Raznik groomed me into a loyal warrior, but he couldn't do that to you. You've kept me from completely losing myself to his ideals, and he wants us gone."

Until this moment, I have never put these pieces together. I have never once considered the chronology of my family and Raznik's actions, and the truth of it hits like a ton of bricks. If he ends our family, he keeps his control without issues. The Pact will remain indefinitely. Our people will never learn the truth.

I retreat inside my head again, trying to come up with a plan. Before long, Willow and Aleca take the lead, and I begin to fall behind. There must be a way other than unreliable magic to keep Aleca protected. I am prepared to take her place as the one to be killed, but I would prefer it not come to that. I do not factor Willow in— I refuse to let anything happen to her. Her only crime is that she is associated with me and my sister, and I won't let her be punished for that. Not again.

"I still want it in writing that magic isn't fake!" Aleca calls to me, breaking my concentration.

"Al, if we make it out of this alive, you can have whatever you want in writing," I promise with a grin.

"I'll be sure to make it good, then."

I carry on mapping and plotting silently while Willow and Aleca continue in front of me. After some time, I realize that it has been too quiet for too long. When I look up, I am alone. I turn wildly, trying to find where Willow and Aleca have gone, but there is nothing but rocks and trees. How long was I in my head?

"Guys?" I call. "Where did you go?" There is no answer, and I call for them again loudly. Still no one answers and I head toward the trees, grumbling at myself for not paying attention and at them for wandering off.

I haven't made it more than six steps when I feel someone behind me. Before I can turn, they let out a roar and I am pinned to the ground. My arms are yanked tightly behind my back, pressing my face into the rocky mud. I attempt to fight them off but cannot move. Through my peripheral vision, I can just barely make out the figure of a woman. A glint of silver catches my eye and I immediately recognize who she is.

"Get off!" I grunt, trying again to throw her.

"I told you that you were playing a dangerous game, ice girl. Your commander wanted you whole, but what's one less Grimme in this world? Only one left now." She leans in close and I can feel her breath, hot and fetid with tobacco, on my ear. "You the one who killed my brother? Heard you talking about him not so long ago. I've been following you on your Commander's orders."

"How the hell should I know? Get off of me!" I freeze when the cold tip of her blade catches at my neck.

"I heard you did. Killed him and left him to rot in the trees of Yolchame. Maybe I should do the same to you."

"Bamet?" I ask. "Is that your brother?"

"Was until you killed him."

"Was until you exiled him," I correct her. She straddles me with a growl, tying my wrists together. The rope burns my skin and I gasp with pain. She has doused it with something and my wrists feel as if they are on fire.

"I'm going to kill you. Sibling for sibling. Only fair, don't you agree?"

"Your brother was a pig and a coward," I spit with as much acid as I can. The effect is somewhat dampened by the mud in my mouth.

There is a fleeting moment of silence before she screams. A searing pain shoots across my right shoulder and into my fingertips as she stabs me. My scream mingles with hers and echoes off of the trees. Twice more, she brings her knife down, and then suddenly she is still. I brace myself for her final blow, but it does not come. Instead, she slides off of me and lays motionless. Blood pools around her head. Frantically, I roll over and struggle to my feet and I look around with wild eyes. Willow stands with a heavy rock in her hands. The rock is slick with blood and she stares at it, dazed.

"Willow?" I gasp.

"I guess I would kill to save someone I love," she whispers, finally looking up at me. She drops the rock with trembling fingers. My heart is pounding in my ears as we stare at each other and I feel myself holding my breath. Neither of us moves until we hear Aleca come crashing through the trees.

"There you two are. Who is that?" she asks, eyes landing on the dead woman.

"Bamet's sister," I say with disgust. "She was trying to kill me."

"She what?" Aleca shrieks.

"Sibling for sibling," I repeat. "Except Willow saved me." I motion to the rock at her feet and hiss in pain. The ropes are still tight around my wrists and have left burns on my skin. Now that the initial fear and shock have worn off, my shoulder burns, and I can feel the blood running down my arm. Aleca takes a knife from her wristlets and cuts through the rope quickly. "Don't touch it," I warn her. "It has something on it."

"Let's get out of here before someone comes looking for her," Willow suggests. "I'll take care of your wrists when we make camp." She wraps a piece of cloth around my neck and arm in a sling and tightly binds a piece of cloth against the stab wounds to stop the bleeding. "All set?" she asks, stepping back. I nod and Aleca takes the lead for us. Willow slips her hand into mine and does not let go.

The ache recedes entirely by the time we settle for the evening. It is not the first time I've been awed by her skill, and it won't be the last. I draw her arm to me as the three of us sit around a fire and draw an image with ash on the inside of her wrist.

"What is this?" she asks, examining it closely.

"Your first tattoo, if you'll accept it," I say, holding up a needle and a wooden stick. "You've earned it." She eyes it for a moment and then hands her arm back to me.

"Do it."

......†......

I have left Willow and Aleca at the camp while they practice their magic together. We are low on food supplies and have another day and a half of travel before we make it into Yolchame. I am gathering more than we need; Willow says I will be welcomed back into the village, but I need to be prepared in case I am not. I do not want to part ways with them if I can avoid it. However, I know they will be safe in Yolchame, and there is no point in putting them in more danger than is necessary at this point. Once we get into Battlewood, there will be more than enough danger to go around.

At last, I cannot carry any more in my arms or pack, and I make my way back to camp. I have found enough fruits, herbs, and vegetables to tide us over until we can find a substantial source of energy. Multiple times, I pass by shrubs of belladonna. The berries are deep blue-purple-black and a tempting sight— if you do not know what they are. Tally's face swims in my mind, and it makes me miss her. I love my sister and Willow but adventuring with them is not the same. There is a hesitation in them that never existed with her. I stare at the berries, wondering what her last minutes were like. Did it hurt? Did she even realize? There is no way for me to ever find out, and the knowledge dredges up an ache in my chest that I have spent months repressing. Could someone in Apaiji connect to the dead? Could I handle that? I do not spare the plants another glance as I march back to camp.

I spend most of the evening absently tracing the belladonna tattooed into my skin. Willow's and Aleca's conversations barely register with me as I sit by the fire. I do not often think about Tally, or about my past, but, when I do, the memories are intense and cause a deep ache within me. Briefly, I think to the juniper mead in my pack. It could calm some of the ache in my chest, dull it. The little that is left would only take me to a slightly less heightened state. Would Aleca and Willow even notice? I glance up across the fire to where they are sitting, talking animatedly. Willow's eyes leave Aleca's for only a moment to meet mine and I flash a warm smile at me.

In that instant, all thought of drinking the ache away disappears. I have worked too hard to fall apart now. This is when I need to hold it together the most. Aleca and Willow need me to be there for them. They deserve to be protected. Despite the bravado that both of them try to put forth, I know their weaknesses and I know how hard it is for them to fight. I cannot desert them now. I concentrate instead on the fire burning in front of me. Part of me is curious to try and see images in the flames; knowing what I do now, I cannot continue to deny the existence of some sort of magic. I think back to the light I held in my hands and try to remember how I made it happen. Desperation, Willow suggested. So what am I desperate to see now? Thoughts tumble through my head all at once. My parents. Tally. Raznik. The future. The truth.

Who I am meant to be.

"Why are you so morose today?" Aleca asks me, poking my ribcage impatiently. We have been walking since first light, but I have said no more than a handful of words in the time between our departure and the rising of the sun that now hangs high above us.

In spite of my best efforts, unwelcome memories and feelings plagued me through the night and I have barely slept.

Resentment and frustration build inside of me, fighting to be free. Until this point, I have managed to keep these feelings repressed. Lately, though, I can feel my resolve weakening. I feel like a fraying rope, and I am struggling to keep myself together for Aleca and Willow. Willow has known better than to push me today; I cannot say the same for my sister. I angle my body away from her hands with an irritated sound.

"I'm not," I say, "I'm just trying to get us somewhere safe."

"You are," Aleca counters. "You have been since you came back from getting food yesterday." She tries to poke me again and I swat her hand away.

"Maybe I'm sick of being out here," I say irritably. The pressure begins to erupt before I can stop it. "It's been months and I'm done with this. I'm ready to be home, and I'm ready to be done with marching through lands that don't want me around. Just because you can't keep your nose out of other people's business, doesn't mean we all want to live like that. I'm not your babysitter anymore, and I'm sick of being forced to be." I'm taking my anger out on her unfairly, but it is too late to go back now.

Aleca's eyes flash angrily.

"I never asked you to be. I'm sorry mom and dad died, and you got stuck with me, but that's not my fault. And it's not like you did a great job anyway. You were too busy drinking and going off with Tally to even care about me. You didn't even think about the fact that it was illegal for you and Tally to be together, or the fact that I could have lost you because of that, did you? All you cared about was you. All you cared about was doing what you wanted. I wish you had never met Tally. She ruined everything."

"I tried my best, Aleca!" I snap. "What do you want from me? I had to be your mom and your dad and your sister all at the same time. I was only fourteen years old! I was hurting too, and I wasn't even allowed to because I had to take care of you and our home. Tally was the only person I could be myself with. She was the only one who loved me for me, not who I was expected to be. I'm here because of Tally! Did you know that I was hurting myself on purpose after mom and dad died? Tally did. Tally is the one who stopped me from hurting myself again, who kept me alive. And then she died, and I still wasn't allowed to hurt, because of you! Because you couldn't see past your own motivations.

"Do you know how much time I spent trying to keep you out of trouble? The same day that I went to the burning of her body, you got arrested and thrown into jail for the first time. Then, you go ahead and get yourself sentenced to execution, and I'm still the one who is being punished for it! You ran away to your precious magic without a second thought, and I was held accountable for it. Tally didn't ruin anything, Aleca. You did. You think I'm selfish? Take a look at yourself."

My chest is heaving as I catch my breath. I'm taking my anger out on her, but I cannot stop myself. All of the thoughts that have been pushed deep down inside of me come roaring to the fore, unstoppable. I can feel a pressure behind my eyes and the unmistakable prick of tears as we glare at each other.

"I'm not sorry that Tally is dead," Aleca says in a low voice. "She was nothing but a drunk and an addict, and she was dragging you down with her."

I take a step back from her as if she has slapped me. My eyes fill with tears and spill over before I even realize what is happening.

"I should have just left you in Apaiji," I say quietly.

"I wish you had." Her tone matches mine. I storm past Aleca, putting several paces between us. I barely make out the sound of Willow saying, "You shouldn't have said that about Tally." I do not wait to hear Aleca's response.

After some time, Willow appears at my side. She does not speak for a long while, instead allowing me to forge a path. Only after I feel her take hold of my arm do I realize that I am crying. Embarrassed, I swipe at my face. She gently wipes away a tear with her thumb and stares at me intently. "Do you need to talk about it?" she asks in her soothing voice.

"Talk about what?" I ask. My voice, mercifully, is steady despite my tears. She cocks her head to the side and gives me a 'you know what I mean' look. "I shouldn't have snapped at her," I say glumly. "It's just…I've never…I've always been responsible for her. Even when she's courts away, I'm the one held accountable. She's right. I wasn't there for her when she was a kid, and I should have been. But I didn't know how to be. I didn't know how to be a parent.

"It was awful. Aleca and I only had each other, and I couldn't do enough for her. Tally wasn't good for me, and I know that, but she saved me from myself. It's thanks to Tally that Aleca still even has me around. It got bad for a while. Hurting myself worked at first, but then that started to lose its edge. I think...I think I may have taken my own life if it hadn't been for Tally." The words, usually so staunchly held back, tumble out of me like they're all fighting to be said first.

"What would have happened if you and Tally had been...found out?" Willow asks tentatively. I can tell she is trying not to scare me back into hiding behind my walls.

"We would have been killed," I say. "Well, no, that's not right. One of us would have had to kill the other."

"Just for loving each other?" Willow asks in horror. I nod slowly, chewing on my bottom lip. "What is wrong with your land?"

I let out a shout of humorless laughter. "More than we have time for," I say. "You know," I add suddenly, "I get it. I get why she left. I can't fault her for seeing Battlewood for what it truly was. It's just...."

"The way she handled it?" Willow offers. I nod silently, slowly scuffing my toe in the dirt. A plume of dust rises and disperses around my foot, and I scuff again.

"I don't...I don't have a place anywhere," I tell Willow. "I'm angry with Aleca, but that's not really…I mean, I just…I don't belong anywhere. I don't belong to anyone. When I was younger, that was all I wanted. I was desperate to be free of answering to anyone or anything, and now…," I trail off, struggling to find the words and feeling foolish for vocalizing my fears. "Aleca belongs in Apaiji. You belong in Garyn. I don't have anywhere to go. Even if I returned to Battlewood, I wouldn't be home. I hate admitting it, but I'm jealous of Al. She knows who she is, what she wants. I'm only just learning that about myself."

"You never stop learning who you are, Jace," Willow tells me. She tugs my arm to stop me and takes my face in her hands. I stare up at her and meet her intense gaze. "You will always have a place with me," she asserts. "If you know nothing else about yourself, know that you will always have a place with me." She wipes the last of my tears off of my cheek with a tender finger, her eyes never leaving mine. I allow myself only a moment before I roll onto the balls of my feet and press my lips to Willow's.

It starts soft and unsure, two feathers brushing together. I worry briefly that I am using her to bury my pain and loss. But then there builds a sort of desperation in the way we kiss, in the way our fingers twist into each other's hair. Everything that has ever gone unsaid makes itself known as my skin comes alive, burning under her touch. When we break apart, she is flushed red and I find it hard to catch my breath. I bring a shaking hand to my lips, and I know that they are swollen from her. Neither of us says anything and instead resume our path. In this moment, though, there is nothing that need be said; there is nothing more that could be said beyond the unspoken promises we have just made to one another.

after the last fall

TWELVE

Aleca and I have not spoken since that night. Several days of frigid silence have passed between us. I have opted to bypass Yolchame on my own, meeting up with Aleca and Willow at the border of Battlewood instead. Willow fights me at first, unwilling to separate our trio. Eventually, she relents and I watch as she and Aleca disappear toward Yolchame. Although Willow glances back several times, Aleca never once turns. Regret fills my veins like poison as my sister grows smaller in the distance. I should have said something, anything, before they left. It was my own stubborn pride— my Achilles' heel— that prevented me from doing so, and now my chance is gone.

For nearly a week, I travel alone. My thoughts vacillate between wondering if Willow and Aleca are safe and wondering just what we are walking into once we have crossed the border back into our court. I have given up trying to predict anything. If I have learned anything since leaving my court, it is that nothing makes sense, and everything changes.

There are no absolutes in life, and I must make peace with that while I can. I try not to let myself get too deep into my head about everything that could go wrong when I return. There are too many unknowns, and I do not do well with the unknown.

The woods and forests are slowly turning back into the lands with which I am familiar. I mark the time that has passed by the crimson and golden leaves on the trees. It is the middle of Autumn. By my guess, I would say that I have been gone for nearly three months, possibly four. That is sure to be a mark against me when at last I am facing Raznik— to be added to the hundreds of marks already against me. At this point, they are meaningless. I am walking around with a target on my back anyway.

To be honest, I have no hope that we will make it out of this situation alive. There are too many factors working against us. Aleca has had a death sentence hanging over her since the moment this began. Willow became an unfortunate target by aligning herself with me. I, by virtue of both my family and my behavior, have made myself no allies within Raznik's circle. It seems insane to me that we are marching willingly to our deaths, but I know that if we did not hand ourselves over, we would be found and killed eventually. We are dead women walking.

There is a large part of me that wishes I had not separated from my sister and Willow. Left alone with my thoughts, I can feel the pallor of despair taking over me again. It weighs in my head and on my chest like chains. I do not know how I ever survived— how I ever stayed out of my own head long enough to remain alive— before I met Willow. Even Tally could not pull me out the way that Willow does. And Aleca…

I have played out our argument in my head over and over again. We both spoke from anger and hurt. The problem with both Aleca and me is that neither of us knows when to back down. It is the Grimme way, and it has been instilled within us well. Neither our mother nor father deferred to each other without a fight. We are a stubborn people, too stubborn by half. It has served me well at times, but this is not one of those times.

Instead, I find myself alone once more.

…… † ……

We reunite the following morning. Willow launches into a description of their travels, which seem to have gone relatively well. They were well-stocked with supplies from both Kydier and Garyn. Willow hands me my own pouch of supplies in a burlap bag. It feels heavy and I sit on a rock to rummage through it. The bag is filled with dried meats and fruits, as well as a new skein for water. Klara has provided me with a mug from Yolchame, the same colorful pottery as her own dishes. I carefully wrap the mug back into the cloth it came in and tuck all of the items back into the bag.

"There was another parcel for you," Willow says, handing me something bulky and wrapped in delicate silk. "It was waiting for us when we got to my home in Garyn. Aleca and I both received something as well."

"It's a gift from the Goddess," Aleca says. It is the first time she has spoken to me since we fought. "It bears her mark."

"Al," I begin.

"I know." It is all that needs to be said between us. We have forgiven one another. We say nothing else, but all of the tension between us dissipates in that moment. I turn my attention back to the silky gift in my hands.

"What were you given?" I ask them.

"A journal," Aleca says. She withdraws a book of parchment bound with beaded twine. A regal white feather is affixed to the front, surrounded by more beaded twine. The cover bears the same mark as my silk: a moonflower. "It's for my notes. I intend to continue my research once I return to Apaiji." There is no uncertainty in her voice that she will return when this is over. Sometimes, I wonder how I am the one who became a warrior, and not Aleca. She possesses so much more self-assurance than me.

"I was given an amulet," Willow says as she draws a leather thong from beneath her tunic. An amulet wrought from ore hangs there, with a clear silver crystal fitted snugly within the metal.

"Were there any messages?" I ask. I do not understand how or why these gifts would be given to us— particularly to me, considering my aversion to gods, goddesses, and magic in general. I fiddle with the twine holding the wrapping shut.

"Just the mark of the Goddess and one line. 'May you persevere,'" Aleca says.

"Which Goddess is this?" I ask as I unwrap my gift. I do not know why I've asked. These gifts all bear the same mark, identical to the one emblazoned on my thumb. Out of the silk flows a swathe of tan and black fabric. I stand and shake it out and a cloak unfolds in front of me. The shoulders are capped with a fur pelt. It has intricate metal clasps to hold it closed, and the inside is lined with pockets. It is the most exquisite piece of clothing I have ever seen, and I get the distinct impression that it is not entirely of this world. A gasp escapes me and I rush to put it on.

"Karishua," Aleca says. "The Goddess of Fate."

…… † ……

It is nearing nightfall when we come to the edge of the border between Garyn and Battlewood. We have agreed to cross the border at first light, when there is less chance of a blind attack. Over the last week that I've been alone, I have created a map of sorts of Battlewood. There were many hidden pathways and entry points that most never knew existed, and I am banking on this still being the case.

I can tell that Aleca is growing frustrated with me as I repeat my warnings over and over, but I will not stop until I am confident that they understand. If what we've seen is true, then we will be captured as soon as our feet touch the soil of our court. If we have to turn ourselves in, it will be on our terms, not Raznik's. I fall silent only after Willow places a hand on my arm.

"We have our plan, Jace," she says gently. "It is time for you to rest. We need to be ready for tomorrow."

I know that what she is saying is true, but it does not put me at ease. How can anyone prepare for their death? I know that there is no point in fighting her, though, and instead, I nod slowly. I rise, rolling my neck side to side as I ease out the kinks. I find myself thinking fondly of the fragrant bath into which Bronwyn forced me just weeks ago. If we make it out of this alive, that will be my first order of business.

"I'm going to turn in, then," I say, making my way over to the tent. I pause as I take hold of the tent flaps and then add, "I want to get into Raznik's quarters. I want to know what he is hiding from us." I do not give them a chance to say anything before I enter the tent and the canvas closes behind me. I know that if I can create some form of diversion, I can get into his quarters. I know how he guards them, and I know his hidden accesses. All that I would need would be something to draw him and his warriors away, long enough for me to sneak in.

Sleep is not to come to me tonight. Long after Willow and Aleca are asleep, I quietly make my way out of the tent and light a small fire. I pace back and forth as it burns, thinking about any scenario with which we may come face-to-face.

There are few that end with us walking away unscathed; the chances of us walking away with our lives are minuscule. Instead of focusing on how we might die, I try to come up with a diversion plan to get me into Raznik's quarters.

At last, as the sun begins to rise, I have a strategy. I wait anxiously for Aleca and Willow to wake. I have barely given them a chance to open their eyes when I begin to talk. For their part, they try to follow along as I speak. I have to repeat myself several times before they finally understand what I am telling them. Both of them begin to argue with me at the same time, and their voices blend together into a mash of unintelligible words.

"Enough!" I cry out. "Listen, one way or another, I'm getting in there. I'd like your help, but if you can't do this for me, I'll find another way. All I'm saying is that I don't think Syiera would have given you the means to do this for me if she didn't know it would come to this." I look pointedly at Aleca.

She stares back at me for a moment, and then lets out a defeated sigh. "She's right," Aleca relents, "and if we don't help her–,"

"She's just going to get herself into more trouble," Willow finishes.

"Thanks for your faith in me!" I cry indignantly. They both raise an eyebrow at me. "Are we ready? We need to make our way down the wall and into Battlewood without being seen."

"We're ready," Willow says, "and we have complete faith in

you." As she speaks, she looks at me tenderly. I feel my heart skip and I try to sober myself.

"Listen," I begin, "I don't know what we are going to find when we get there. We've made a lot of enemies in the last few months. Raznik wants us dead, and there is more than one warrior who would be willing to deliver us to him on a silver platter. It's not too late for you two to turn back. I…I wish you would, to be honest." I look away from them, a lump forming in my throat. "You're the only two people in the world who matter to me. I'm going to do everything in my power to keep you safe, but—,"

"We're coming with you," Willow says. "You matter to us too."

"You're out here because of me," Aleca adds. "I'm not letting you go down for me. We go together." She and Willow stare at me with a steely determination in their eyes and I swallow down my tears.

"Then what are we waiting for?" I ask. "Let's go home."

...... † ......

We travel through the day, night, and into the early morning before finally stopping to rest. Aleca and Willow sleep uneasily, but I still cannot bring myself to sleep. I am on edge and trust nothing. We are too close to the end, and I find myself wishing that I was back on Talolyn's ship, or back at Syiera's gardens, anywhere but here. More than once, I need to wrap my arms tightly around my torso to prevent myself from breaking down completely. The pressure forces me back to reality and I focus closely on my breathing. I am running on pure anxious adrenaline at this point, and I say little as we continue our trek.

We weave in and out of trees quietly and carefully. There are guards posted on the perimeter of the forest, though they look uninterested in much more than sleep. Twice, I could swear that we are seen. I make direct eye contact with two different warriors and I hold my breath as I wait for the attack that never comes. When I mention it to the others, Aleca suggests that my cloak has glamoured us.

"And what exactly is a glamour?" I ask.

"You know, an image spell. Something that makes you look like something or someone else. Maybe your cloak is magicked to do that. I mean, it's from Karishua," Aleca says with a shrug. I stop to consider. If this is true, and my cloak is more than it appears, I will worship Karishua until my dying breath. I am unwilling to test this theory more than is necessary, however, and we continue our careful journey toward the castle, stopping frequently to take cover as guards meander nearby.

I request to make a detour before our final destination. As we clear the last of the forest and make our way up the mountainside, the land becomes more and more familiar. I am not excited—as I once thought I would be—to see the land. I feel an odd sort of longing for what I do not miss but know that I should.

Before long, we are back in our village. The large stone

fountain in the center is crumbling and a steady leak has wetted the ground around it. A gnawing feeling begins to eat at my stomach and I touch the weakened stone nervously. Battlewood has changed in the few months I've been gone, that is irrefutable. I allow myself one more moment before trekking to the other side of the village. When I reach our destination, I let out a gasp; beside me, Aleca makes a wounded sound.

"Our home...," she whispers.

I stand outside of the rubble that rests where our home once stood, staring in horror. The charred wooden beams have begun to mold and disintegrate. This has the work of Raznik written all over it. Hate rises in my throat and my eyes sting with anger. Raznik has taken everything that belonged to me or my family and destroyed it. That Aleca and I got out unscathed is nothing short of a miracle. I walk through the still-standing outline of the door and into what was, at one time, our living room. A dark pewter pot still hangs in the brick hearth, and more pots are strewn around the floor. There is hardly anything left of the home we grew up in, where we made our memories. Flashes of Aleca and me as children sitting at the hearth while our parents read stories to us come to mind, and I rest a hand on the burned mantel sadly. Nothing is as it once was.

I wander through the debris, kicking aside stray pieces of beams and stone as I do. Moss sprouts in the shadowy parts of the ruins where the sun has not managed to completely dry the wood, stone, and rotting books. I can make out the basics of where Aleca and I shared a room, where my parents slept, their office. All of it is warped and ruined, a despairing end to the life I once had. For just a moment, I think I see something glowing in the corner, but as I approach it, I see nothing but more shadows and mold.

I turn to look at the rest of our home. Aleca is on her hands and knees, sorting through half-burned books. Willow helps her sort; she goes through the books looking for any pages that may be salvageable. I make my way toward the back of the house, toward the room where Aleca and I were never allowed as children. Mother and father always told us that it was because it was too boring for energetic girls like us but I have the distinct feeling that they were hiding something. Everyone has their secrets, it would seem.

The only thing I am able to rescue from this room is a metal box locked with a chain. I cannot begin to imagine what this could be, but I am not willing to leave behind a single item from my home. It is— was— the last place I belonged, and now I am truly adrift.

"I'm done here," I announce as I rejoin my sister and Willow. "We should get moving."

They both rise, shuffling the papers that they collected and stuffing them into Aleca's journal. We are changed girls from the ones who lived here so long ago, and the tension in this room stretches taut like a band between us, ready to snap. One way or another, this ends today.

THIRTEEN

All too soon, we come to stop on the outskirts of the cavernous mountains that lead back to the castle. We make our way across the rocks and begin the ascent, leaving the trail partway through. From here, there is a complex underground tunnelway that leads to various parts of the castle. It is dangerous; the karstic mountains are unsteady and could crumble at any time. It's a risk that we have to take, though. We make our way through the labyrinth of tunnels, footsteps echoing off the walls. We are all panting by the end and a sheen of sweat covers all of us.

"This is it," I say. "Once we're clear of this tunnel, we're in the castle." I unclasp my cloak and hand it to them. Willow takes it uneasily. "One of you needs to wear this. If it really is glamoured, you'll be safe. It'll help you with the diversion. Get out if you can, but don't do anything stupid."

"Like breaking into Raznik's quarters?" Aleca asks. Despite her attempts to tease me, I can hear the shake in her voice.

"Right," I agree. I pause and then grab her into a hug. "I love you, Al. I'm so proud of you, and I'm proud to be your sister."

She squeezes me tightly, and mumbles into my shoulder, "I love you too, Jace."

I hear her sniffle, and I place a kiss on the top of her head before letting go and turning to Willow. "Willow, I…," I stop, unable to say the words. They hang there, unspoken.

She fills the void by placing her hands on my face. "Be safe, Jace," she implores me.

They leave the tunnel before me. There is a shout and then an explosion. It is my cue, and I sprint out of the tunnel and through the chaos. Guards and warriors take no notice of me as they rush past to the source of the noise and, in moments, I skid to a stop in front of Raznik's quarters. I take one deep, steadying breath, and then give the massive doors a push. They creak open and I step inside tentatively. "No more lies," I whisper.

I set to work immediately. I overturn his books, rummage through the drawers in the desk, and pull the cushions off of his couch. Belatedly, I remember the image he drew on the floor beneath the carpet and I begin to roll the heavy material away. When I finish, I come face-to-face with the same image I watched Raznik create when we were with Syiera. I let out a sound of triumph and make my way to his desk.

I have pulled out every single drawer and emptied them of their contents. I cannot find the papers I saw, though, and I rifle through them hurriedly. I am about to take them all and hide them inside of my tunic when I hear the doors open. My heart and stomach turn to lead.

"Well, well," an oily voice says behind me, "what have we here?" I close my eyes in dread and slowly turn around.

"Ocin," I say through gritted teeth. An anxious fear twists itself tightly around my lungs and stomach. This would not bode well regardless of which warrior found me here, but there is no love lost between Ocin and me. We have opposed one another since the beginning. There is a special kind of hatred that arises in warriors who do not get along. Ocin and I, who were trained together, found any excuse to pound on one another and try to hold the other back. I have been on the receiving end of his fists too many times to count and I swallow hard, knowing what is coming. He was cruel, even as a young trainee. I can't imagine what he has become since then.

"Grimme," he says with poorly-contained glee. He eyes me up and down as he considers our positions. "Long way to fall from the top, innit?" he continues. "Only now, I get to be on top. And you…you get to take whatever I give you." He grins a brutal grin and runs at me. I throw the papers in my hands into the air as I dodge him and they scatter to the ground. Ocin misses me only by a hair's breadth and I feel the wind around me as he rushes past. He catches himself on the edge of Raznik's desk and turns to face me quickly.

"Look, I'll go with you," I say, putting my hands up. "You've got the upper hand here, I get it." He charges me again and I stumble backward. Stuck between the edge of the fireplace and the wall, I have nowhere to go. I duck but he catches a clump of my hair in his hands and pulls. A stinging pain races across my scalp and I let out a yelp.

"You think I'm letting you get away that easily?" he asks me. I can smell the faint musk of sweat on him and watch as droplets roll down his forehead and into his eyes. He slams me against the wall and the force of it presses the air out of my body. "You shouldn't have come back here, Grimme," he hisses into my ear, a hand wrapped around my throat. "Everyone wants you dead."

"Then kill me," I rasp. My voice is compromised by the pressure he has placed on the center of my throat. I try not to move too much in order to preserve what precious little air I have left. "That is, if you think you've got what it takes to kill me." He licks his lips as he watches my face turn red.

"Don't think I haven't thought about that," he tells me, bringing his lips to my ear, "because I have. Every day since I got stuck with you. But I'm not taking that away from Raznik. If that's what he decides to do with you. Personally, I recommended torturing you. You remember our sessions? I'd volunteer again." Ocin's breath, hot on my ear and neck, send me spiraling back into memories of our trainings, and my stomach flops. He runs the tip of his tongue against my earlobe once, slowly, and then drops me suddenly. I double over, gasping greedily for air.

"I knew you didn't have it in you," I mutter as I massage my neck. In an instant, I feel something sharp in the center of my back and I slam into the ground. I curse myself for my inability to keep my mouth shut as my face comes into contact with the marble floor and my lip splits open. I roll around and onto my back. "What the–!"

I am cut off by Ocin bringing down a fireside poker onto my left temple. The last thing I see before my vision goes black is the sight of his boot aiming for my ribs, and then there is nothing.

······ † ······

When I open my eyes again, I am laying on the floor of the dungeons. Aleca and Willow stand above me, peering nervously into my face.

"Willow, she's awake!" Aleca hisses. "What on earth happened to you? The last time we saw you, you were in one piece and doing fine. Then suddenly Ocin comes dragging your lifeless body in here and leaves you bleeding in a heap! Are you okay? Did he do this to you? Did he do anything else to you? You'd tell me, right?"

"Aleca," I whisper hoarsely, "I need you to just…" I trail off and stare up at the ceiling of the dungeon, taking slow breaths in. My ribs protest every single movement but I ignore them. "Just hush." I lift a hand to my head and delicately touch the place where Ocin hit me. It is sticky with blood that has not quite dried and causes a deep, throbbing pain in my head. Willow watches warily.

"There is little I can do for you right now," she tells me. "I can bind your ribs if you'd like, but there is no water to clean your wounds." She begins to tear away strips of her long skirt without waiting for my answer, and then slowly helps me sit up.

"Ocin found me in Raznik's quarters," I tell them. "I don't know how he knew I'd be there, but he did. And…well, you know how much we've always hated each other," I say to Aleca. "He saw his chance to get the upper hand on me for once, and he took it. I probably shouldn't have goaded him, but…" I trail off again as Willow lifts my bloodied tunic to wrap my ribs tightly. "Are either of you hurt?"

I examine them, noticing for the first time that Willow is sporting a black eye. Aleca shakes her head though.

"We made it out alright. Willow called one of the guards a really nasty name— honestly, I didn't think she even had it in her—and he knocked her one, but other than that, it went pretty much how we expected. They left us well enough alone, although they did take your cloak," Aleca says apologetically. "Honestly, I think they were all just too tired to push. You should have seen them, Jace. They looked like they hadn't been fed or allowed to sleep in a week."

"Knowing Raznik, they hadn't. It's his favorite training tactic. Ocin took my diamond blade from me too. I hope he stabs himself with it," I say bitterly before letting out a groan in pain.

Willow makes a repentant sound and then pulls my tunic back down. "All better?"

"You look like shit," Aleca says.

"Thanks, Al," I say flatly. I scooch myself across the floor until my back is against the wall and let out a sigh.

"So?" she asks. She and Willow come to sit beside me. "What did you find?"

"Not much," I admit. I quickly regale them with my search of his quarters. As I speak, I can hear myself growing disheartened. It feels like a wasted effort that resulted in nothing more than broken ribs and an aching face. I take stock of the three of us. We look like the motliest crew of vagabonds in existence. I nearly laugh at the fact that the three of us are trying to overturn Raznik. There was never a more unlikely trio than us, and we fit together like a poorly formed puzzle.

We lapse into a silence and sit huddled together. I watch as water drips from the ceiling and into a puddle on the ground. I cannot tell what time of day it is. I begin to drift off when I hear the sound of whistling and approaching footsteps. Ocin's face appears on the other side of the gate. His eyes land on me and he grins.

"The Commander has ordered you to speak with him in the chamber," he says, opening the door to our cell. The iron screeches as the hinges swing wide. None of us moves from where we are seated. "Move it, prisoners."

"And if we refuse?" I ask. Ocin lunges forward and grips me by the arm, ripping me to a standing position. He grabs my wrist to yank my arm up and behind me and shoves me against the wall. He places all of his weight against my body, rendering me motionless. The feeling is familiar and terrible and I want to throw up. My jaw bounces hard off of the wall and I feel the rough rock scrape against my skin. My ribs ache at the sudden pressure. Behind him, Willow and Aleca shout out in protest.

"We can do this my way or the hard way," he hisses in my ear. "Do either of you want to argue?" he adds over his shoulder.

"No, sir," Willow and Aleca say quickly.

"Smart girls," he says. "Desnal, lead those two. I've got this one."

"Sir," Desnal says.

"How's your head?" he asks me with a laugh before he forces me around, keeping my arm tightly behind my back. We are led to the chamber where Aleca's hearing was to take place, where this all began. When we enter the chamber, the benches are crowded with an audience. Valkyrie Elouned stands at the center with Raznik, conferring. She has her sepiwin in her grip, and my mouth goes dry.

"We haven't been brought here to speak, have we?" I ask.

"Time's up," Ocin says. "You had a good run, Grimme, but you're too much trouble." Louder, Ocin calls, "Sir, the prisoners."

"Ahh, Jace Grimme. My old friend!" Raznik calls. He extends his hands toward me, but does not take a step forward. I have seen the transformation Raznik has gone through since I left, but seeing it in person still shocks me. Gone is the well-coiffed man who led the court; in his place stands a wild beast, eyes alight with violent glee. Elouned stares me down with bloodthirsty eyes, her lips pursed. I look around quickly, trying to find a way out or anything that can be used as a weapon, but there are no options. For once, I feel truly trapped. I struggle against Ocin's grip anyway, trying to shake myself free. I can feel his hand growing clammy around my skin.

"Some friend," I spit. "What do you want from us, Raznik?"

"Oh, I think you know what I want," he says. "Your heads, on my wall." The crowd laughs at that and I glance up at them in disbelief. These are the people I once called my friends and family, and I cannot believe that I could have ever found comfort in them. "Ocin, you may release her. Even she is not stupid enough to try something when the odds are so stacked against her."

Ocin drops my arm and I groan in relief, massaging my aching shoulder. I can feel Willow and Aleca move to flank me, and we all link hands. We present a united front, regardless of what happens to us. We stare him down, waiting for someone to make the first move.

"You've come to the end," Raznik tells me, "all three of you. This land does not breed traitors or witches. There is no room for lies and deceit. There is no room for treason."

"Then why are you still here?" I ask coolly, raising an eyebrow. "Because if I'm remembering right, I've seen you use battle magic." His lip curls in a snarl and he balls his hands into fists at his side. "You pretend that magic has no place in Battlewood, that it shouldn't exist at all. But I've seen magic, Raznik. I've been through the lands that you claim are our enemies. We are the real enemy. You are the enemy." I hear murmuring on all sides as the audience listens raptly. Raznik looks around, taking in the sudden shock and confusion in his people. He is standing on a precipice, and he has to do something before it gives way.

"She would have you think that magic is real!" Raznik says to the crowd, laughing. "We signed the Pact of Silence one hundred years ago. Our ancestors knew that the lands around us were corrupt and dangerous. You are proof that they continue to be corrupt. Listen to you, shouting about the existence of magic, decrying your own people! You are a black mark against your court."

"Why did we enter the Pact, Commander Raznik?" I ask quietly. I can feel sweat— my rage sweat, as Aleca has always called it— beading on my forehead, and heat rushes through me. I fight to keep my anger in check as I stare across the room at him. "If you're going to kill us, you can at least have the courtesy to give us some answers."

"Magic is a stain on the tapestry of our people," Raznik

growls. "The falsehoods that our surrounding courts tried to spoon-feed our people caused strife and despair. There is no room for worshipping false idols! You have worshipped the Commanders before me, and will continue to worship us as your rulers. We will not have dirty blood in our lands. We will not allow the imperfections and filth to seep into our grounds and poison the minds of everyone here!"

"You try so hard to keep everyone under your thumb, Raznik, but you're losing your touch," Aleca says. "Look around you! People don't know who to trust anymore! I've seen what's been happening behind closed doors. Battlewood no longer believes in you. You've lost your way as their Commander."

"You–!" His face twists with anger.

Before he can continue, I cut in, "Why don't you bring our people to your quarters? Shall I tell them what they would find? A casting circle and a book of battle magic?"

"Relics from those before us," he says, waving a hand. "Your arguing begins to bore me." Raznik fakes a yawn and then turns to face all sides of the crowd. "People of Battlewood, we have a choice to make. Do we spare any? Do we kill them all? Or," he says, turning a cruel eye to me, "Do we command Jace Grimme to kill the two spares?"

I am reminded of that very first hearing where I listened to my people decide the fate of my last living family. My rage begins to build, and it is only moments away from bursting through the dam in my chest.

"Kill the spares! Kill the spares!" A war cry, echoing across the walls and into my ears, rips from the crowd. My mouth goes dry as I remember my dream in which I killed my family.

"Bring me the Garyn girl," Raznik commands, beckoning with two fingers. Elouned wordlessly hands him her weapon as Ocin takes hold of Willow and begins to drag her forward. She looks over her shoulder at me, her eyes wide with terror. My heart lurches excruciatingly in my throat.

"Jace!" I can hear the fear in her voice. There is a buzzing in my ears as I try to come up with some type of diversion. Distracted by Raznik's gleeful look and the way he fingers the blade covetously, I cannot think of a single thing. I give another desperate glance around the room for anything to stop him before he can kill her.

"Raznik, you don't have to kill her!" I shout at him.

"But Jace," he says in mock surprise, "I'm not going to kill her. You are." He holds out the sepiwin to me.

"Your problem is with me, not with Willow!"

"She became my problem the moment she allied herself with you," Raznik said. "And what better way to punish you than to kill someone you love? What was the name of that other girl? Tally Ash? I would have thought that after her death, you would have learned your lesson better than this."

Aleca inhales sharply beside me. I feel the air whoosh out of my lungs and my hearing turns to a buzz in my ears. I realize with horror that Tally didn't kill herself. She was murdered. Dizziness overtakes me and I fear I may fall. Aleca pinches the inside of my arm hard and after a moment, I can stand straight again. My heart thuds furiously in my chest and I renew my search for a weapon. Tears of anger blur my vision and I shake them away, taking a shuddering breath. I want him dead.

"Looking for something?" Aleca whispers, nudging my left leg. When I look down, the empty sheath is no longer empty. The diamond blade has found its way back to me.

"Magic," I whisper, "thank the goddess for magic." I rip the blade out of its protective cover and let out a shout. Raznik's eyes widen as he realizes what I hold.

"Seize her!" Raznik screams, the picture of insanity, spittle flying from his mouth. The dam in my chest breaks and white-hot anger spills from the tips of my fingers into my blade. The guards move toward me, but not fast enough, and then the weapon is out of my hand and soaring through the air before I am even aware of my plan. It is as if time slows down while I watch the blade glint as it flies. Its trajectory is sure and straight, and it meets its target dead-on. With a sickening noise, the diamond blade burrows itself deep within Raznik's chest, blood immediately staining the cloth around it in a deep crimson bloom. He stares at me with wide, accusing eyes as he falls to his knees and then topples forward. The blade sinks deeper into him as he lands. He does not stir.

I walk over to him, turn him over, and dislodge my weapon

from his still body. The diamond blade drips with his blood as I crouch beside him. "Expect no mercy, Commander," I whisper softly.

······ † ······

The cacophony that follows the death of Raznik is instant and overwhelming. In a fit of childish anguish, I drop into a crouch, cover my ears, and squeeze my eyes shut.

"Loud, loud, loud," I repeat over and over as I press down hard on my ears. I cannot quell my anxious mantra as the world carries on around me. Although it muffles the sounds around me, it does little to erase the image of Raznik's corpse before me. My feet squelch sickeningly against the ground in his blood. It is all that I can do to keep from vomiting at the sight and smell. With Raznik dead, the guards have halted their movements. They have just lost their commander and have no one to answer to anymore. I have just taken the life of their leader. Elouned has vanished entirely; that will be an issue for another day, I fear.

Aleca and Willow rush toward me, fighting against the sea of people who have begun to race toward Raznik's body. The din is deafening, and all that I can make out are their concerned faces trying to reach me. Exhaustion has caught up with me, and I drop to my knees. My body aches and I cannot bring myself to move. It is too much for me to handle, and I let out a scream. I expect it to be drowned out in the chaos around us, but instead, the entire chamber falls silent. In that moment, the mark on my arm— my mysterious tattoo— begins to burn red hot and I let out a shout of pain.

"Jace?" Willow asks in concern. "What's wrong? What is happening?" She and Aleca drop down beside me, their arms shielding me from those around me. I feel a comforting weight as Willow places my cloak around me once more.

I clear my throat and swallow hard. My throat, raw and dry, prevents me from speaking. Before I can answer, another voice comes from behind me.

"What are your orders, Commander Grimme?"

after the last fall

EPILOGUE

The moon has risen high into the sky when I make my way outside. I have no idea of the time, but judging by how few houses are lit, it is very late. My breath comes out in small puffs and I tighten my cloak around me. Autumn is in full force and the days continue to grow colder. I do not look forward to the first snowfall, but I know that it is only a matter of time. There is so much that needs to be done before then. So many answers to find. There is no map Talolyn could ever create that would guide my hand in this new journey.

My feet lead me without waiting, and soon, I find myself in the thicket of trees behind our funeral pyre. The leaves have begun to fall off of the branches, and the topmost branches extend into the sky like skeletal fingers. I have not been back to these trees since Tally's death. My eyes are drawn immediately to the shrouded cove of shrubs where I found her after her overdose. After her murder. I crouch beside it and sink my hands deep into the cold soil. My eyes flutter shut, and for a moment, I feel as if she is there with me. The feeling does not last, though: she is gone and I am entirely alone. I rise again and continue my walk.

The path I follow is one I've walked countless times before. I know it almost as well as the lines on my hands. There are exactly eight boulders, twenty-two trees, and three forks in the path. Each boulder has been marked in some way by me, Tally, and the other two who we used to run with before trouble came and we parted ways. I pause by each stone, running my fingers along the engraved words and symbols. At the very last boulder, I lower myself to sit on my knees, bringing myself close to the warped and weathered stone. The mark is faded, nearly rubbed away, but it is still there. It still boasts the promise that Tally and I made to never stop defying the odds— no matter what they were. It's a promise that now only I can make good on.

I root around for a scrap of parchment in my cloak and withdraw the letter Raznik sent me weeks ago. Despite the horror it still brings me, I have not managed to bring myself to destroy it. It will serve a purpose now, at any rate. I place the parchment against the symbol and rub dark, damp soil against it. The symbol may be fading from the rock, but it will not be lost forever. It is one of the few ways I have left to honor the memory of Tally and all of the other innocents who have lost their lives at the hands of Raznik. At last, I rise and make my way back to the castle.

······ † ······

The days that follow in the wake of Raznik's death are marked by confusion, chaos, and exhaustion. I have every desire to crawl into myself, and no ability to do so. Battlewood demands answers; the only problem is that I do not have them to give. Any semblance of stability that Battlewood maintained under Raznik's descent into madness has been erased completely. Everything is a mess, and I do not know what to do. Willow and Aleca seem to think that I will find my way. I do not share their optimism. I rarely do.

I have been left reeling in the aftermath. I did not plan to be alive right now. I did not plan to usurp the commander of our court. I did not expect to discover that the accidental death of Tally was a murder, or that my parents' deaths were murders too. Battlewood has been turned upside down— I have been turned upside down— and now it is my duty to fix it. As someone who is unable to fix even the smallest issues without some form of trouble getting in my way, my hopes are not high. I do not have much of a choice, however, and that is how I come to find myself sitting in the middle of Raznik's floor, staring into the fire as Aleca and Willow sit beside me.

"I need to make some sort of structure," I say, watching the flames scorch the wall behind them. "Raznik was losing his hold for a while, but no one knows what to do. They don't want to follow his edicts, but they don't want to trust an ex-criminal either. And the other courts do not know that there has been a change of hands. I want them to. I want to end our Pact of Silence. I want our people to know what is truly out there."

It's a risk, I know, but I cannot continue to conceal what I've learned to be true. I will not allow our people to remain in the dark any longer. The mistrust between courts must come to an end. For too long, we have been misled. It is time to fix what Raznik, and his family before him, destroyed.

"You're asking for a lot of changes, Jace," Aleca says slowly.

"No. I'm not asking," I say, finally tearing my gaze away from the flames. "I am telling you that as Commander of this court, changes are coming. We will not live in the dark for another moment."

...... † ......

Acknowledgements

Creating this book was an absolute labor of love, and I could not have done it without the incredible people who stood with me.

First, I'd like to thank Anna Sansom for editing After the Last Fall, and for patiently pointing out each and every time Jace furrowed her brow or raised an eyebrow.

Second, I'd like to thank Leah Kent for designing the cover of my dreams, and for nerding out with me over fonts and calligraphy; I'd also like to thank Leah for letting me be picky about specific fonts and sending me over four even better examples than what I could have suggested.

Third, I'd like to thank Nicola Humber, owner of the Unbound Press, for taking a HUGE chance on me, and giving me the honor of being the first-ever fiction book under the Unbound Press, building me up and encouraging me to expand this beyond what I could have imagined, and for letting me share my novel with the world.

acknowledgements

I would be remiss if I didn't thank a few very specific people in my life, as well.

To my parents, thank you for always encouraging me to write and patiently reading every single short story about dolphins and magic as a child;

To my sister, Colleen, thank you for helping me network with local stores and plugging my novel, for helping me with my fundraising events, for creating a launch party for me, and for being a sounding board for the design and plots;

To my sister, Elizabeth, thank you for sharing my journey with your circles, for supporting me on this journey, and for being a sounding board for the design;

To Kathryn Casella, who has been my writing partner-in-crime for the last 15 years, who vlorred (yes, I know it's a fake word) with me to help figure out plot points, and who graciously gifted me the character of Bronwyn;

To Mrs. Olshewske, my first grade teacher and the spark behind my love of writing, and who ALSO put up with countless stories about dolphins and magic;

And to my partner, Sarah, who has been my greatest cheerleader, my partner in this journey, my support and motivation, and who gave me enough courage to reach out to Nicola in the first place. I love you more than the sun, moon, and stars.

About the Author

Having been writing since the first grade (so many stories about dolphins), this is the first novel I've written start to finish and dared to share with the world. There are several other projects in the works as we speak.

When I'm not writing, I work as the coordinator of my local LGBTQ Center, as an advocate for victims of domestic violence, and as an accountability educator for perpetrators of domestic violence. I try to imbue my work into my writing-my greatest hope is that I can remove stigmas around mental health and inspire people to be their most authentic selves.

I am one of the co-hosts of the podcast Queers on a Couch, where one of my dearest friends and I talk sassy about all things LGBTQ!

I live in the Finger Lakes Region of New York with my partner and my spoiled rotten furry babes (seriously. My cat Milo has his own Instagram page (@HRHMiloJames)).

I can be found on Facebook under Amy Babiarz (there aren't very many of us), or at my website, acbabiarz.wordpress.com.